In the Herriot Room, Dr. Mac handles the ducklings, turns them over and makes comforting little clicking noises at them. She works slowly and checks each of them from bill to tail. One after another, she places them back in the stainless steel box on the exam table. I've put a towel in the bottom of the box. Dr. Mac says that they'll have firmer footing that way. But none of them is doing anything but lying still and breathing.

"Brenna, it's a good thing you kids found them. All three are weak. And this last one," she says, holding the one I was worried about, "is in very bad shape. Let's get them some water first."

Dr. Mac prepares a shallow dish of cool water with a little sugar mixed in. The ducklings stick their bills into the water, lift their heads slightly, and slurp it down right away. But the one we're most worried about does not. Dr. Mac makes a note on her chart.

I whisper, "You can do it." The duckling just blinks. Then it dips its bill into the water and drinks. Yes!

Collect All the Vet Volunteers Books

LAURIE HALSE ANDERSON

VET VOLUNTEERS

Treading Water

PUFFIN BOOKS
An Imprint of Penguin Group (USA) Inc.

PUFFIN BOOKS
Published by the Penguin Group
Penguin Group (USA) LLC
375 Hudson Street
New York, New York 10014

USA / Canada / UK / Ireland / Australia / New Zealand / India / South Africa / China

penguin.com
A Penguin Random House Company
First published in the United States of America by Puffin Books,
an imprint of Penguin Young Readers Group, 2014

LIBRARY OF CONGRESS CATALOGING-IN-PUBLICATION DATA IS AVAILABLE

Puffin Books ISBN 978-0-14-241678-5

Printed in the United States of America

1 3 5 7 9 10 8 6 4 2

Chapter One

· · · · · · · · · · ·

I click the remote, and my next wildlife photo brings "Aww"s from the audience. It's a good photo of the cutest kit—or baby fox—ever. I turn away from the screen to face the Ambler High School Outdoor Club. The twenty students are all older and way cooler than the kids at my middle school. This classroom is bigger than any we have there. Even the AV equipment here is amazing. They have a projector system that hooks right up to my computer, and it was super easy to figure out how to use. So the flip-flops of my stomach aren't over the unfamiliar equipment but the unfamiliar audience.

I didn't expect to be so nervous. My older brother, Sage, went here for four years, plus the high school is just on the other side of the parking lot from the middle school, so I'm familiar with the building. But today, it seems like a whole different world. I gave this presentation just last week to my middle school's Environmental Club, but over there, it was like talking to a bunch of first graders. A few of the boys kept playing with a globe every time the faculty adviser left the room—which was way too often. They'd take the globe off the stand and toss it around like a basketball. Some of the girls thought this was funny and egged them on. Others pretended not to notice and whispered back and forth to their friends. Even my friend David goofed around with his buddy Bruce. Nobody really listened to me, I barely got through the presentation, and we didn't get much else done at all.

So I jumped at the chance to be able to speak to older, more civilized kids. I thought I'd be just fine talking to students who are only a few grades ahead of me. But now that I'm here, I'm worried that I look like a little kid. I'm worried they'll think they shouldn't have invited me. And that my photos aren't good enough to show. I take in a deep breath. At least I know they'll like this one.

Focused pale-copper baby-fox face in the foreground and spring-green grasses in a perfectly blurred background. I hear a few more "aww"s from the back of the room. If they like this one, wait until they see the next one. I click.

Cheers and claps erupt. This photo is one of my best. I used to take pictures on my phone's camera, but one day my dad told me I had a "good eye" and surprised me with a real camera. The pictures I can get are so much better than the ones on my phone. I've saved money and bought special lenses to get even better shots. And I'm still learning.

In this photo, three fox kits tumble in the grass as the sunlight turns the tips of their copper fur bright orange. It's as if each one is being chased by the sun. As action shots go, it's a winner. I feel myself blush. I don't want to seem too full of myself, but everyone wants to talk about this shot.

"Brenna, did you just sit out there all day to get that picture? Like, did you know they were gonna play like that?" a boy in front asks.

Before I can answer him, the girl beside him asks, "Yeah, were you lucky, or are the kits that comfortable around you?"

I think a moment. "A little of both," I begin. "To get wildlife shots like this, I do a lot of waiting. A lot of sitting. Or leaning. Or balancing in weird positions alongside streams, and cliffs, or in trees. I'm learning to wait for good lighting. And I wait for the wildlife to appear."

I take a sip from my water bottle and continue, "But in this case, I didn't want the kits' mother—who, remember, is recovering from a broken leg and is stressed out—to see me. So I sat behind the enclosure. . . ."

I click back to an earlier photo to remind them of the setup we have at our family's wildlife rehabilitation center. I stop at the one that shows the small wooden coop with the high chicken-wire fencing around it.

"When I'm sitting behind the coop, the mother can't see me, but she can keep an eye on her kits. I'd been watching several afternoons, and I knew that this was an active time for the kits. I had clipped some fencing to stick my camera lens through—I didn't want the chicken wire in the shot. I paid attention to the sunlight, and I was ready when the sun was at this fantastic angle to really light up those kits. So yes, to answer your question: it was both. Lucky that they were out tumbling in the clear late afternoon. But I had already put in plenty of time paying attention to the sun and to where the kits liked to play. So I was ready to get lucky. Does that make sense?"

Heads nod. A boy in the back shoots me a thumbs-up. This is so cool. I'm enjoying this presentation much more than I expected. When the Ambler High School Outdoor Club asked me to speak on the Save Our Streams Cleanup Day that I organized with my fellow Vet Volunteers, I was not sure I wanted to do it. High school kids can seem so, well, intimidating. But then, Maggie Mackenzie, Dr. Mac's granddaughter and one of my best friends, said she'd do the presentation with me. We came up with my slide show. We made notes about who would talk about which part of that day. And Dr. Mac even let us borrow some of the equipment from her veterinary office. I have examples of bandages, splints, and Edwardian collars—otherwise known as cones— that Dr. Mac uses with injured animals. Maggie was supposed to talk about all that.

But Maggie called last night and told me her teacher said she had to stay after school to retake a test.

"She's giving me a second chance for a better grade. I can't pass it up," Maggie had explained.

I wasn't happy, but I couldn't blame her. It was too late to get Sunita, David, Josh, or Jules to step in. And Zoe already had plans to go shopping. So here I am. Just me.

I'm not feeling nearly as nervous now. It's so much easier talking to kids who don't fool around and who actually listen. A girl dressed in a tie-dye shirt and a long skirt has a question. "Do you get to play with those adorable foxes anytime you want, or are there only certain times of the day that are okay?"

"Oh no, we're never allowed to play with the animals," I say.

She looks surprised. "Well, I don't mean actual playing, I guess. But handling?"

"Those fox kits are healthy. It's their mother who needed medical care. So she does have to be handled occasionally. Her wounds have to be checked for healing. We have to be sure she isn't showing signs of infection. But we try to observe her as much as we can to assess her health. Only when we absolutely need to do we handle her."

"Are you afraid she would bite you?" asks tie-dye girl.

"No, it's not that. We don't want her to get too used to humans. We expect to release her back into the wild. And that's even more true for her kits. If they became tame, they might be in danger in the wild."

"And why is that?" another girl asks.

"They'd be likely to approach people. Which would make them more likely to get hit by cars, or to get shot at by people who assume they're rabid. It's safer that they remain as wild as possible when they're in our care. So we keep out of their sight. They're confined in this pen with their mother, but we do everything we can to be invisible to them. Even when we bring food, we don't let them see us. We don't want them to associate people with food."

"I never thought about that," tie-dye girl says.

I glance at the clock. I have only a couple minutes left, and I want to present one more idea before I go.

"We're hoping to have another Save Our Streams Cleanup Day in late summer. Maybe some of you would like to volunteer?" I suggest. I hold up the handouts that I've prepared with the details of our Environmental Club that meets at the middle school. The handouts also have my blog address and bullet points about the next Save Our Streams Cleanup Day.

Nick, the one who invited me to speak, and the president of the club, speaks up. "I think we oughta do it as a club. It's certainly in keeping with our mission." He picks up the stack of handouts and starts passing them around the room.

"I'm in Philadelphia this summer doing an internship," one boy says.

"And I'm a summer exchange student in Denmark," the girl in front of me says.

"I'll be working full time at the Dairy Bar," says another.

"Come on," the flannel-shirt boy by the door says to the girl beside him. "You won't work twenty-four hours a day at the dairy." He turns to me. "Is it a weekend sort of thing? An all-day commitment? How long will it take?"

"With enough volunteers, it only takes a half day. We've done it twice, both times on Saturdays. That seems to work out for most people."

Flannel-shirt boy raises an eyebrow at the girl who's working at the Dairy Bar. She nods her head yes. He winks at her, and she blows him a kiss. I feel my face flush again. I don't know why I'm blushing. They're the ones flirting with each other in front of everyone. And yet, I'm both embarrassed and curious. Weird.

Exchange students in foreign countries. Internships. Full-time jobs and boyfriends. High school is so cool. More and more, my classmates seem babyish to me. I can't wait to be done with middle school. High school is going to be great.

"Let's give Brenna Lake a hand," Nick says.

I feel a rush of relief and a burst of energy. This went so well I could skip. Do cartwheels. But I won't. Because that would be babyish.

Nick continues, "Thanks for spending time with the Outdoor Club." The students clap and get ready to go. Some stop to say thanks as they file out the door. Some sign the volunteer sheet Nick has just made for the stream cleanup. A couple students stop to talk to me.

"What did you do about the hole in the fence?" the boyfriend of Dairy Bar Girl asks.

"The hole in the fence?" I ask.

"Didn't you say you cut a hole so you could get that great picture?" He pulls Dairy Bar Girl in and puts his arm around her shoulders.

"Oh, right." I turn off the projector and start powering down my computer. "Yeah, I had to patch that before my dad noticed. The fences are patched in a bunch of places around our wildlife rehab center."

"You should do your slide show for the Photography Club here," Nick says joining us. "They're meeting every afternoon next week. It's their Blitz Week."

Dairy Bar Girl nods. "My best friend, Najla, is president. She's always looking for presentations to do on their non-shoot days."

"Photography Club? Cool." Now I really cannot wait to go to high school.

"Give me your number, and I'll have her contact you," Dairy Bar Girl whips out her phone and puts in my info.

"See you around," she says as she and her boyfriend maneuver out the door, still connected at the shoulders.

On my way out, I ask for directions to the school's auditorium. I have a plan beginning to form. And it wouldn't hurt to see this space again. I take a quick look at the stage and the amount of seating. I check out the school's cafeteria, too. Just in case. Then I head outside.

The spring air cools my face as the doors close behind me. The light breeze feels much better than the overheated high school. I scan the parking lot for my brother Sage. His battered Camry usually sticks out. But not in a high school lot. Looks as if almost everyone drives a beater. Sage might be running late. His last class at community college doesn't always end on time. If I didn't have my computer and the box from Dr. Mac, I could have walked home. I set everything down on the sidewalk at the side entrance to the school. It's where we agreed to meet.

At the far edge of the parking lot, a few students are gathered and looking intently at something on the ground. I can't see what it is. As a group they move slowly as if they are surrounding something that is also slowly moving. My curiosity gets the better of me. I grab my computer and the box. What can it be?

I cross the parking lot to find out.

Ducklings. Three yellow, fluffy ducklings waddling slowly and hardly peeping. Looking closer, I see that only two of them are peeping. The third follows along behind and occasionally trips. It isn't making any noise. I don't know a lot about ducklings, but I do know they should be much louder than this.

"Brenna, what do you think?" It's Nick from the Outdoor Club.

"Where did they come from?" I ask. "There shouldn't be waterfowl out here. There's no water for miles."

A tall girl stoops close to the lead duckling. "They were just here when I came out to my car. I was afraid somebody would drive over them. So I've been trying to, well, herd them. Keep them safe." She uses her foot to stop the lead duckling from going any farther. It stops. So the other two do, too.

Nick crouches down, and the duckling scoots backward. Nick stands. "Oops. Didn't mean to scare it. Should we just leave them here? Do you think their mother is here somewhere?"

We all scan the parking lot and the school's running track beside it. A couple kids check between the parked cars. Nick and a few others race toward the middle school parking lot that's right next to this one. After a thorough check, it's clear: there is no mother duck. There is no place for another duck to hide.

"I think they're abandoned," I say. The other students agree.

That's when Sage pulls up. I hear his car before I see it. "Whatcha got there?" he asks from the open car window.

"Abandoned ducklings." I open his car door and drop my computer on the backseat. Then I carefully empty the contents of Dr. Mac's box and put all of her equipment on the backseat, too.

"Grab a duck," I say to Nick as I scoop up the fragile-looking one, then a second, and place them in the box. "We'll take them to Dr. Mac's Veterinary Clinic to get checked out."

Nick puts the third duckling in the box. He holds the box while I scoot into the passenger seat and buckle up.

"Let me know how they're doing," Nick says to me as he hands me the box of ducks. And to Sage he says, "You oughta get that muffler fixed. Not good for the environment."

Sage nods, and we're off to Dr. Mac's vet clinic with this box of fluff, too-quiet peeps, and quick-blinking eyes.

Chapter Two

. . . .

In the Herriot Room, Dr. Mac handles the ducklings, turns them over and makes comforting little clicking noises at them. She works slowly and checks each of them from bill to tail. One after another, she places them back in the stainless steel box on the exam table. I've put a towel in the bottom of the box. Dr. Mac says that they'll have firmer footing that way. But none of them is doing anything but lying still and breathing.

"Brenna, it's a good thing you kids found them. All three are weak. And this last one," she says, holding the one I was worried about, "is in very bad shape. Let's get them some water first."

Dr. Mac prepares a shallow dish of cool water with a little sugar mixed in. The ducklings stick their bills into the water, lift their heads slightly, and slurp it down right away. But the one we're most worried about does not. Dr. Mac makes a note on her chart.

I whisper, "You can do it." The duckling just blinks. Then it dips its bill into the water and drinks. Yes!

There is a knock at the door, and Dr. Mac's granddaughter Zoe walks in.

"Hiya, Brenna. Hiya, Gran. What's in the box?" Zoe asks. Before we've answered, Zoe is peering in. "Ohh, so cute," she squeals.

"Cute and sick," I say.

"Perhaps not sick," Dr. Mac says. "They may just be dehydrated and hungry. Let's get another bowl of water ready."

"They were abandoned at the high school," I explain to Zoe. "At least we think they were abandoned. No mother in sight." I stir a quarter teaspoon of sugar into the tiny bowl.

"Why don't we just get one of the cat bowls for them?" Zoe asks, touching the adorable tiny webbed feet of one duckling. "We wouldn't have to refill so often. I could go grab one for you."

"That would be dangerous for these ducklings." Dr. Mac says. "They might get into the bowl and try to swim."

"So?" she asks. "They're ducks. Maybe they'd feel better with a swim."

"They could drown," I explain. I run my finger along the biggest one's back. "See how they don't have any feathers yet? It's just downy fluff. Not water repellent. If the bowl was bigger, they could get in and they'd get waterlogged. They might not be able to get out, and they'd drown right in their bowl."

"Oh, wow. That's terrible. But I know I've seen little ducklings swimming before. Maybe not in real life but in the movies or on TV," Zoe says. She scratches her head as if she's trying to come up with the movie's title.

Zoe knows her movies and TV shows. Her mom is an actress, and Zoe has spent a lot of time around actors in New York City and in Hollywood. Now her mom is filming in Canada, which is why Zoe—once again—is living with her grandmother and cousin, Maggie. Maggie, Zoe, and Dr. Mac live in the house attached at the back of the clinic.

It's fun having Zoe around, even when she is going on and on about fashion or cute guys.

Dr. Mac swaps the water bowls out. The ducklings drink, but not as fast as they did with the first bowl. She says, "I'm not an expert on ducklings. We'll have to do some research. But I imagine the presence of the mother duck keeps ducklings safe. But we have no mother duck. Brenna will have to fill that role."

Dr. Mac smiles at me, and I nod. I'm happy to help.

Dr. Mac continues, "Brenna, I imagine your family has handled abandoned ducks before?"

"Grown ducks, yes. But I can't remember us taking care of ducklings before. I don't have experience with them."

"Want to call your mom or dad for us?" she asks.

Before I can call home, Nick from the Outdoor Club is at the door with Zoe's cousin, Maggie. Nick holds a box. Maggie stares into it, her brow furrowed.

Beside me, I hear Zoe quietly say, "Ooh, cute." She is talking about Nick, of course. Zoe never misses a chance to flirt with a good-looking guy.

"Hey, Brenna," he says. "We found one more. It was hiding underneath one of the cars. It doesn't look so good. A couple of us did a thorough search under the rest of the cars. This is it. No more baby ducks. No mother."

Dr. Mac crosses to the door. Zoe is right beside her and manages to get between Nick and Maggie. Maggie looks at me and shrugs. We know Zoe, after all.

"Oh dear," Dr. Mac says. She takes the duckling from the box and lays it on the exam table. It is folded over onto its side. Its legs are pulled up under it, and its webbed feet look like claws. Even though the other ducklings look weak, none of them looks this bad.

Dr. Mac examines this duckling just like she did the others. All of us gather around the exam table and watch. When Dr. Mac looks in the duckling's mouth, she whispers, "No."

Then she opens a drawer beside the exam table and pulls out some long tweezers. With one hand Dr. Mac carefully opens the duckling's bill, and with the other she inserts the tweezers. The duckling just lies there. No movement but the chest moving slowly up and down. No noise at all. Dr. Mac draws the tweezers out, and something long, shiny, and stringy is pulled from the duckling.

"What is that?" Maggie asks.

"That is Easter basket grass," Dr. Mac says.

"Oh! These are abandoned Easter gifts," I say. I immediately feel sick to my stomach. People can be so reckless with animals.

"I don't get it," Nick says. He is still holding the empty box. "Some little kids got live ducks instead of marshmallow ones?"

I nod. "Instead of letting the Easter bunny just bring a basket of jelly beans and chocolate, some parents also give baby bunnies and chicks. And baby ducks, obviously. I hadn't considered it before. But Easter was only a week and a half ago, and we've already found boxed chicks and bunnies on the doorstep of the wildlife rehab."

Zoe's eyes are huge. "Wait a sec. So parents give their kids a pet then take it away a few days later?"

"And who thinks a baby chicken is a pet? They shouldn't, anyway." Maggie adds.

"It's true. Every year we get people's cast-off animals. Every year my parents wish they could do something about it." I look at the faces around the examining table and then down at all the little ducks. Everyone is quiet. Even Zoe

"Well, I gotta get going," Nick says to me. "You did a great job today. I'm sure I'll see you around school. I'll probably stop in when you do your presentation for the Photography Club."

"Thanks," I reply. "You know, I was thinking I'd like to join your Outdoor Club."

Zoe raises an eyebrow and stares at me.

"Oh," Nick says, crossing his arms. "I don't

know if you can. It's for high school kids. Someday, right?" He smiles and nods.

Why do I immediately feel five years old?

"I can walk you out," Zoe says. Her eyes are sparkling, and her face is pink.

"Not necessary," Nick says. "See ya."

"That guy is awfully cute." Zoe says as soon as Nick leaves the room.

I reply, "He's president of the Outdoor Club. I spoke to his club today."

"And you want to join it, I see." Zoe turns to Maggie, "Weren't you supposed to do that, too?"

"Yeah, but I had a test to retake," she says to Zoe. She looks at me with a sad smile. "How did it go?"

"Great. They were friendly, and they loved my photos, especially the one of the kits tumbling, and you wouldn't believe how much nicer their school is, and all the great clubs they—"

"Girls," Dr. Mac interrupts. "Let's finish with our patients first."

I feel bad. For a moment, I forgot about the reason we were all standing here. We help Dr. Mac get another stainless steel box and towel.

She fills a small, needleless syringe with some fresh sugar water and gently squeezes the plunger with one hand while cradling the duckling in the other. Dr. Mac presses slowly to give the duckling some hydration. We've all done this ourselves after Dr. Mac trained us. Usually, it's kittens that need this special treatment. We want to be sure the sick or hurt animal can actually swallow, so we don't drown them. If the animal cannot—or shouldn't—swallow, Dr. Mac gives the animal hydration through an IV. This little duckling is swallowing. A tiny bit. It's going to be time-consuming to fully hydrate it.

"Want me to take over?" Maggie asks. She puts her arms out, and Dr. Mac hands her the nearly limp, little yellow bit of fluff. Maggie is amazing with animals. I sometimes forget that she's just one of us Vet Volunteers and not someone who has already gone to vet school.

"Thank you, Maggie." Dr. Mac leads the rest of us out of the exam room and back to the recovery area.

I look around at the cages and containers for animals we need to keep overnight or longer. Animals that have had surgery or just need watching before they can go home to their families are cared for in this big back room. In the farthest corner, Dr. Mac sets up a heat lamp in a recessed stainless table.

"We'll put the ducklings here for now," she

says. "I'm hoping your folks will take them to the rehab center as soon as they're healthy enough."

"I'm sure they will," I say. "We don't have too big a census right now. Some chicks, lots of bunnies, an owl, a raccoon, turkeys, maybe a turtle, still, and a fox family." Census is what we call the number of animals we have at any given time. Sometimes we have recovering deer, skunks, raccoons, and, of course, birds of every kind. We've even rehabilitated an eagle. And a very special crow.

The clinic doesn't have a very high census today, either. There is a German shepherd in one of the largest cages by the door. He's wearing a plastic cone around his neck to keep him from getting to the bandage on his leg. On the other side of the recovery room, a couple of cats in high cages sleep. That's it. Sometimes Dr. Mac has so many animals we have to improvise with carrying crates. But today, it's pretty quiet.

After we set up and test the heat lamp, Dr. Mac checks on the cats and the German shepherd. When she isn't speaking softly to one of her patients, she talks to us. Dr. Mac believes in teaching and reviewing everything that goes on in her clinic with the Vet Volunteers. This means diagnosing and treating patients as well as cleaning and sanitizing every surface. Sometimes It feels as if we spend way more time cleaning than actually working with the animals. But I know from our family's center that keeping everything clean is important. Germs slow down healing. And can make an injured or sick animal worse. It doesn't mean I like to do it, though.

Zoe and I mop the floor. Dr. Mac wipes down the tables. She checks a couple of cupboards and counts some supplies. Maggie first brings in the box holding the lone duck, and then returns with the other box holding the three ducks. We all watch as the three ducks settle beneath the heat lamp in the one box. In the other box, the lone duckling just lies on its side.

Zoe asks, "Should we put them together? Maybe this one would get better quicker with its friends?"

Dr. Mac shakes her head. "We need to keep them separated until we know for sure what's going on with this one." She points to the little one on its side.

"But you took out the Easter grass," Zoe says.

"True. But there might be more wrong with it. Or there may be more plastic grass in its system. Better to keep them apart until we know for sure.

I'll do my overnight check on them all, as usual. And tomorrow, if this little one is better, we can consider putting them all in the same box." Dr. Mac ushers us out of the recovery room.

In the waiting area, Maggie, Zoe, and I tidy things up. Well, Maggie and I do. Zoe flips through a magazine and squeals.

"Look at this dress on her!" Zoe holds the page to show us some actress on some city street. "Don't you think Selena wore it better on the red carpet? Just last week. I can't believe that Shailene wore it, too."

Zoe doesn't actually expect us to answer. Maggie smiles at me as Zoe flips another page and continues babbling on about somebody's clothing.

It's clinic closing time, and my mom is here to pick me up. She talks to Dr. Mac for a minute as Maggie, Zoe, and I turn off the lights and restack the magazines. I'll be back tomorrow morning for our weekly Saturday Vet Volunteers meeting.

"See you tomorrow," Maggie says as I head out the door with Mom. "I still want to hear about the Photography Club's invitation. I promise I'll be at that one!"

I wave to the cousins. The high school students wanted to see more of me, my photos, and my photographic techniques. They invited me back for another presentation. They didn't ask for Maggie, but I ought to bring her anyway. But not Zoe. Zoe would be distracted by all the high school boys. And I would be definitely distracted by boy-crazy Zoe. I wonder if the Photography Club would let me join them?

Chapter Three

· · · · · · · · · · · ·

Sunita unlocks the clinic door for me and relocks it behind me. The clinic won't open for an hour and a half. Sunita is always the first one here for our meetings. She's the most organized of all the Vet Volunteers. She takes meeting notes even though Dr. Mac has always said it wasn't necessary.

"It helps me listen better," is Sunita's reasoning. I'm glad she takes notes. Sometimes I need to go back and read them, especially if I was a little busy taking photos of the other Vet Volunteers or our patients.

I usually bring my camera wherever I go. There is so much to see, and sometimes I see it all better through my viewfinder. Maybe it is a little like Sunita's note taking; taking pictures helps me focus on the details of what I'm really looking at. But that's likely to be whatever is around me and not always whatever it is that Dr. Mac, or Dr. Gabe, is saying.

Dr. Gabe is the other vet in Dr. Mac's practice. Dr. Gabe mostly handles the stable calls. Stable calls aren't just for horses. It's what we call all vet visits to farms and even to my family's wildlife rehab center. Large animals are usually involved: horses, cattle, pigs, sheep, and goats. But a stable call can be for a newborn lamb, which is about the size of a cat, or for birds, like the eagle that my parents kept in our critter barn until he was healed. Dr. Gabe is often at our Vet Volunteers' meetings, but not always. So far, nobody is here today except Sunita and me.

"Dr. Mac filled me in on your ducklings," Sunita says, picking up a clipboard. I like that she called them my ducklings.

"Do you think you'll keep them, or even one?" she asks. "Would Poe Crow be jealous?"

Edgar Allan Poe, my pet crow, has been with me for a while now. He was shot by a hunter, and we rehabilitated him at the center. But he can't fly anymore, and that means he wouldn't survive in the wild. So I was allowed to keep him. Poe comes with me almost everywhere. He even rides with me on my bike. I've never met anyone else with a pet crow.

But I know—after a lifetime with my parents—that, with the exception of Poe, none of the animals we care for are mine.

"I'd love to keep the ducklings," I tell Sunita. "But when they're all better, we have to release them back into the wild or find safe places—sanctuaries—for them to live."

Sunita nods. "I just thought that maybe this time would be different."

"I wish. As cute as they are, and as much as I would love to raise and keep them, I know it's not in the cards," I say. "What is it with cute animals? When we release them, Mom and Dad seem so happy and I always feel sad."

Sunita nods again. She is such an understanding friend. "You always have your pictures, at least."

"You're right," I say. "I'll be sure to get some good ones of the ducklings. I should probably snap some fresh shots of Poe, too. I can add them to my high school wildlife presentation. Maybe I'll even bring him along. Do you think I'd have to get special permission from the school?"

Sunita leads the way to the recovery room. "I think you would."

"But I bet the students would love him," I suggest. How could they not?

I can hear the ducklings as soon as we enter. We head to the back corner and the glow of the heat lamps. In the first box, the ducklings drink and peep and move around a lot more than they did yesterday, their webbed feet kicking up the pine shavings in the bottom of the box.

"Dr. Mac and I switched out the towel for the shavings," Sunita says. It's like she read my mind. "Dr. Mac said she went through seven towels last night and early this morning."

"That's because ducks poop every fifteen minutes," I tell her. "They're pretty messy animals. I researched with my mom last night. They've cared for ducks before, but it's been a while. I brought my findings to share with everyone today." I wave the paper I have folded up in my hand. Sunita nods. We look in the second box.

The lone duckling doesn't look any better. In fact, I think it looks worse. I don't see any shavings beneath it, just a towel like we used yesterday afternoon.

"Why didn't you switch this one to shavings?"
I ask Sunita.

"Because he's stayed pretty dry. Hardly any pee
or poo. Dr. Mac is worried about that," Sunita tells
me. "She says it means he's not eating or drinking
enough."

Sunita checks the chart hanging from the table
ledge. We can see that the three ducklings are eating and drinking pretty well. We can also see that
the lone duckling received a syringe of water from
Dr. Mac a half hour ago. If they poop every fifteen
minutes, there ought to be some evidence of it
on that towel. Sunita and I look at each other. She
doesn't look hopeful. And I don't feel it.

Someone is knocking on the clinic's glass door.
I hope it's our friends and not an emergency pet
problem. Sunita and I go back out front. David
is horsing around with Josh. We let them in and
Josh's twin sister, Jules, follows behind. She nods
her head in the direction of the boys and rolls her
eyes. David and Josh together can be a lot of fun.
But they can also be a pain. Sometimes David,
especially, has a hard time knowing when to get
serious about things.

Jules pats my shoulder as she walks by, "Just
wait till you see what they've come up with this
morning."

Sunita raises an eyebrow. She relocks the door. Dr. Gabe, if and when he gets here, has his own key. And the rest of our group will arrive from the back, through the long hall that leads to Maggie, Zoe, and Dr. Mac's home. We gather in the waiting room and wait. I take a candid picture of Josh and David fist bumping. When I try to do the same of Sunita and Jules, Sunita ducks and Jules puts on a cheesy smile. That won't be a good shot.

The dogs arrive first. Maggie's old hound, Sherlock, paddles in, followed by Zoe's peppier, sweet mutt, Sneakers.

I hear Zoe before I see her.

"How will you ever know if you like parsley breakfast shakes if you never try them?" Zoe asks.

"I'm not drinking anything green," Maggie says to Zoe before sitting down on a couch and waving to me. Zoe sits beside Maggie and shakes her head. I take a quick photo of them.

"I put pears in there, too, you know. And you like pears," Zoe insists.

"Yeah and I like Pop-Tarts better." Maggie's tone seems to signal the end of the discussion.

"Good morning, everyone," Dr. Mac greets us. Even though she is Maggie and Zoe's grandmother, she sure doesn't seem like a grandma. Dr. Mac doesn't look or act old like a lot of grandmothers do. I've seen her lift heavy animals. I've seen her climb fences. And she can run fast when she has to. Dr. Mac is pretty cool. I hope I'm like that when I'm her age.

"Look at this, look at this! I'm practicing for a campout with my dad," David says. He pulls a small flashlight from his pocket, turns it on, and pretends to lick it.

"What is that supposed to be?" I ask.

"Yes, what is that?" Sunita asks.

"I'm having a light snack! Get it?" David says. He laughs so hard he tips over.

We groan. Even Josh.

We hear a key in the door. Dr. Gabe walks in with a stack of files. Zoe is up in an instant and across the floor.

"Need help?" she asks. Zoe rests one hand on Dr. Gabe's arm.

"Hi Zoe, no thanks. I've got it," he replies. He smiles and nods in our direction. "Hi kids, Hey, J.J. I have a few cases to go over with you before I finish these files."

J. J. MacKenzie is Dr. Mac's real name.

She says, "I've just begun with our hardy volunteers. Should be about ten minutes. Then I can take a look."

He nods and smiles at Dr. Mac. He smiles down

at Zoe. Zoe smiles, pivots, and returns to her seat with a goofy expression on her face. I think Zoe imagines that Dr. Gabe treats her special. But actually, cute Dr. Gabe treats everyone like they're special. Little kids, old folks, all of us, and of course, all the animals. Sometimes I get frustrated with people and the way they can be with animals. Dr. Gabe is patient and understanding. He shows people how to care for animals. I'm not sure that even if I wanted to be a vet I could be one. I get mad too fast. My parents are always trying to show me how to handle myself in these situations. And Dr. Mac has reminded me more than once to chill out. But how do you do that when things—people— need fixing?

Dr. Mac resumes our meeting. She makes checks on her clipboard as she talks. "So, gang, I have Maggie, Zoe, Brenna, Sunita, and Jules on cleaning crew for tomorrow. David and Josh have duties at the FFA horse-judging contest. Have a great time, you two. And tell us all about it next week. As for today, the exam rooms, surgery, and recovery rooms are cleaned and ready. We need only our usual quick clean of the waiting area. David and Zoe, could you water the plants? And Sunita, I could use you at the desk for about ten minutes. Josh and Jules, I have you down for glass cleaning. We have even more canine noseprints on the doors than usual. Brenna and Maggie, can you mop? We'll all meet up in the recovery room for a duck exam. Brenna, do you or your parents have info to share with us about duckling health?"

I whip out my paper. "Got it right here."

"Perfect," Dr. Mac says. "I knew I could count on you."

We all get to work. I take a few pictures of everyone at their tasks. At one point, Maggie stops mopping and stares at me with her hands on her hips. I get the picture. Too much camera work, not enough mop work. I press the lens cap back onto my camera and grab my mop. We really are done fast. Fifteen minutes later, all of us—including Dr. Gabe—are gathered around the duck boxes.

It is a terrible, sad sight. The little lone duckling is dead. It's obvious even before Dr. Mac pulls out her stethoscope to check its vitals. The duckling is on its side. It's still, legs curled up, webbed feet clawed. Her eyelids are half open. An animal that has died just looks like an empty place.

I feel my temples throb. I am more than just sad. I am so angry. Furious, really. This didn't need to happen. I take a picture.

"What are you doing?" Sunita cries.

"I . . . I just wanted to document this," I reply.

Sunita's eyes are wide and her mouth is open. She looks shocked, horrified. I horrified her.

"I just don't think it is right," she says. "What will you do with that picture?"

"Jeez, Brenna," David says, "Not cool."

"Well, I don't know," I say. I really don't know. Why did I take that picture? I think I just reacted. But is it really such a terrible thing to do? To take a picture of an animal that is dead? Don't we have to see and remember bad things, too?

My face is hot. I must be as red as the heat lamp. The rest of the Vet Volunteers look confused. It's hard to read what Dr. Mac or Dr. Gabe thinks.

"Sorry?" I try.

Finally, Dr. Mac speaks. "I'm sure Brenna will be respectful, whatever she decides to do."

It's like the air has come back into the room. I look at Sunita. She does not look at me. She places a towel over the dead duckling. Is she keeping me from taking another picture . . . or just being respectful to the duckling?

The other ducklings are peeping loudly. Maggie and Josh put on gloves, and Jules picks up the duck-lings chart. Dr. Mac demonstrates how she exam-ines the ducks, and Maggie and Josh do the same. We are all supposed to follow along, even though we don't each do an exam. Dr. Mac wants to teach us, but she never wants to overhandle a patient. We can learn by watching. I'm having a hard time paying attention. I wonder what everyone thinks of me. I'm still not sure that I did anything wrong. But other than disaster photos, like birds caught in oil slicks, I can't remember seeing pictures of dead animals before. Not in a magazine. Not in a gallery show. Maybe I did do something wrong.

"Brenna?"

"Brenna?"

I realize that someone is talking to me.

"Sorry, yes?" I say.

"Did you want to share your duck research with us?" Dr. Mac smiles and nods.

I feel encouraged. Until I glance at Sunita. She still looks spooked. I try a little smile in Sunita's direction. Her brow furrows. I better begin.

"I talked with my parents and I Googled a bunch of stuff. The most important thing to know about ducks is that they don't have any saliva." I see Dr. Gabe nod agreement. He must know a lot about ducks because of his farm calls.

I continue, "So they always need a water source. Food can get stuck in their mouths or throats, and they can choke and die if they go without water."

Maggie jumps in. "So these ducklings would probably all have died if you hadn't rescued them from the parking lot. There isn't any water near the high school, is there?"

I shake my head no. There is no water there. Rescued. I think Maggie is trying to make me sound heroic in front of the others, especially Sunita. But of course, somebody else would have found them and probably taken them to Dr. Mac's or to the rehab center. At least, I sure hope that would have happened. I don't want to imagine it any other way.

"Other duckling facts: They are very messy. Ducks poop about every fifteen minutes." I pause to see if David is going to make some kind of joke, but he's serious for a change.

I flip my paper over and read: "It's hard to tell the gender of ducks until about seven weeks—"

"Seven weeks?" Jules interrupts. "That seems like an awfully long time. How can you tell at seven weeks?" Jules looks at the ducklings as if she might be able to tell right now whether they're boys or girls.

"At about seven weeks, the ducks are fully feathered," I begin. "The males have some tail feathers that curl back toward their heads. The girls do not. Oh, and also, girls quack and boys whine."

"Boy ducks don't quack?" Josh asks. "Are you sure?"

I shrug. "That's what my parents and my research tell me."

Dr. Gabe confirms this. "Right now these ducks are so young that they just peep. But we might be able to tell from their vocalizations before they're fully feathered. Because, yes, only the girls quack."

"What kind of whine do boys make?" David asks.

"A whispery whine," Dr. Gabe says. "Like this." Dr. Gabe makes a noise that sounds like a cross between a frog and a pouting toddler. We all laugh.

I continue with a few more duck facts. Yesterday, Dr. Mac, Zoe, and I talked about how ducklings weren't water repellent. I share this information with the others. They need to know about the dangers of drowning for little ones like this.

Dr. Gabe points out that the ducklings are starting to form wings. There is a definite angle or elbow to them. I don't remember seeing that yesterday.

Dr. Gabe leans on the table and looks closely at the birds. "They look pretty good, don't you think, Dr. Mac?"

Dr. Mac says, "They do, indeed. They've made a fairly rapid recovery."

Sunita shakes her head and asks, "Are we sure

they'll be okay? That whatever killed the one duckling won't kill them?"

Dr. Mac looks at Sunita and then down at the
ducklings. "We can't be sure, yet. That's why we'll
keep them here a little longer. But the one duckling
was severely dehydrated. And of course we know
it had ingested some plastic grass. The combina-
tion was just too much for one so young."

Sunita nods.

Dr. Mac pats her shoulder and says, "It's always
hard to lose a patient, Sunita. We'll be watching
the other three carefully."

Everyone is quiet for a moment. And then Dr.
Mac hangs the ducklings' chart up.

"Do either of you know what breed they are?"
Dr. Mac looks first at me and then at Dr. Gabe.

I shrug my shoulders. I didn't find out enough
about ducks last night to figure that out.

"I'm just taking a guess here," Dr. Gabe begins.
"We won't know definitely until they feather out.
But I think they're Pekins."

"Perkins?" David says. "Like the pancake place?"

"Pe-kins," Dr. Gabe enunciates. He straight-
ens and leans back. "They're non-native ducks.
Naturally flightless. Often sold at feed stores and
tractor-supply places. So it's not like they'd be
separated from their mothers. They would have

hatched in a brooder and shipped. Of course, we can't know for sure yet. But since Dr. Mac found the Easter grass in this one's throat," Dr. Gabe gestures to the covered duckling and continues, "I would guess somebody bought them for their kids without thinking about the care they would need."

"And then decided they were too much work and dumped them!" I say, a bit too loudly. The German shepherd with the leg wound barks.

Maggie goes over to comfort the dog. She pets him and says, "Shh, shh, shh."

Sunita slowly shakes her head. "The people who abandoned them most likely did not know what kind of work they were getting themselves into."

"That's no excuse," I say. "They were careless to buy them. And then to dump them! They could have brought the ducklings here. Or the Ambler animal shelter. Or to us. My family would have cared for them. This one did not have to die!"

The shepherd barks again. Maggie sits down on the floor beside its cage and pets him. The ducklings stop peeping. I think I scared them, too.

"Sorry," I say.

"Well, it's about time to open. Josh, Jules, and Zoe, you're on today. I'll see some of you tomorrow and the rest of you during the week when you're scheduled."

"Do you want me to stay a little while and file?" Sunita asks Dr. Mac.

"Oh, could you? You wouldn't mind?" Dr. Mac replies. I swear they go through this every week. Sunita offers, and Dr. Mac always accepts and thanks her over and over again. Dr. Mac hates the paperwork part of running a vet office. Sunita loves putting things in order. It all works out.

I take a picture of the remaining ducklings. I thought Sunita would have liked that. But instead, she looks at me curiously and walks out the door.

Dr. Gabe pats me on the shoulder. "I heard your folks agreed to take the ducklings. They look almost ready to go. Couple days, I'd say."

"We'll be ready," I say.

"Hey," Zoe says at the door, "I hear you're doing another talk at the high school. I'll come along and help. Just tell me when. I can hold things up like the game-show girls do."

Zoe demonstrates by running her hand down the doorframe like it's a prize. She smiles extra big and bats her eyelashes. She kicks her foot behind her and says, "Or I can pass things out, serve refreshments, whatever." Zoe bounces out the door.

Maggie is petting the shepherd back to sleep. She shakes her head at her goofy cousin. With her pinky and her thumb, she forms a pretend phone and puts it to her ear, mouthing, *Call me.*

I nod. But I don't really want to call Maggie when I get home. Because as much as I'd love to have her help me at the high school, I know Zoe will get on and want to talk about helping. And I don't want to have to say one more I'm *sorry* today.

Chapter Four

. . . .

At our rehab center, Mom and I prepare a duck enclosure in the critter barn. We haul out a stock tank. It's a six-foot-long, flat-bottomed, oblong basin of galvanized steel. It's about two feet high. This might seem like a lot of room for three little ducks, but they'll need room to grow. We use stock tanks for baby chicks and young turkeys, too. We secure—as best we can—a screen of chicken wire on top to keep raccoons and other animals out.

Mom brushes back the hair from her face. "We'll have to take the ducklings out of this tank a few times a day for exercise. We'll walk them around the barn, but we'll need to keep them clear of our little fox family. We wouldn't want the foxes to frighten them. Oh, and we'll need to steer clear of our raccoon, too."

We set up a heat lamp but keep it turned off. We put plenty of wood shavings in the bottom of the tank. Mom sets a big flat stone in there as well.

"What's that for?" I ask.

"We'll put their water jar on it. Setting it up higher will help keep the shavings out. A little. They are such messy birds."

"That's putting it mildly," I say. "They sure go to the bathroom a lot."

"A whole lot, plus they're energetic drinkers," Mom says and laughs. "Come on, we're done here. Let's check on our other critters."

I follow Mom around the critter barn, cleaning and feeding. We have five bunnies that are not from the wild. More abandoned Easter pets, I'm sure. They all showed up on different days this past week. At least people didn't dump them in a parking lot. But still, what are people thinking? What's wrong with giving your kid a fuzzy toy bunny instead of a live one that they aren't ready to take care of?

We check water bottles and the tiny hayracks for the bunnies to be sure they're filled. The bunnies are so cute. Mom and I pick up each one and handle it. Since they're pet bunnies and won't be released into the wild, it's important that we keep them tame by petting them.

Mom nuzzles the little Polish bunny in her hands. It's a soft gray bundle of fluff with tiny sticking-up ears. "Originally, I was going to take them to the animal shelter on Monday," she says. "But the manager tells me they're overrun with rabbits right now."

Some years we've had as few as three after-Easter rabbits dropped off here. And the shelter has been able to take them. But other years—like this one—the shelter has too many of its own and can't take ours. In the past, Dr. Mac has called some of her patient families to see if they wanted to adopt a bunny. I wonder what we'll do this year.

When we're finished with all the animals inside, we do a quick check on the outdoor animals. The fox family appears to be napping. The healing, tail-less raccoon on the far side of the rehab center is also sleeping. Everything and everyone seems A-OK.

We walk by my dad's quiet workshop. He's delivering and installing a whole kitchen's worth of cherry cabinets. He's been working on them for months, and everyone is glad his long hours have finally come to an end. The money will be nice, too. After all, Sage is in college, and college is expensive.

We continue on into the house—it's really more of a cabin. It's cozy and beautiful. I know that when I grow up and have a place of my own, I'll want a cabin like ours.

My little brother, Jayvee, is lying on his belly in the middle of the kitchen floor, partially under a chair. He has a stack of small square papers and a half dozen or so origami dinosaurs strewn beneath the table and chairs. He is roaring so loudly for his dinosaurs that he doesn't hear us come in. I swoop down and pick up the closest one and "Raaarrrrhhh!" at him.

Jayvee startles and bumps his head on the underside of the chair.

"Oh dear, sorry, buddy!" I say.

He stands, blinks quickly, and rubs his head. I think he's trying not to cry.

"Sorry, sorry, sorry," I repeat. I start to hand him the dinosaur, until I notice that I've crushed it. I must have damaged it when he got hurt. I guess that startled me.

"Sorry. Let me fix it," I say. I try to smooth and flatten the parts that look like they should be flat, and re-crease a couple other spots.

"You've ruined it," Jayvee says. He takes it from my hands and refolds.

"You know I didn't mean to do that, right, Jayvee?"

"This is a Dimetrodon. It was really hard to make. You should be more careful," he says.

"You're right. I was just trying to have some fun with you," I say.

He looks at me suspiciously.

"Really," I say. "Looks like you've fixed it. Good as new."

He holds it up for me to see. It's obvious it's not good as new.

Mom ruffles his hair. "She didn't mean to wreck it. Now, let's get this cleaned up."

Jayvee shoots me another look.

"Sorry," I say, one more time. This sure has been a sorry-full day.

"Hey, Jayvee, how about if we set up your dinosaurs outside in the grass and rocks, and I'll take pictures of them?" I suggest.

"Why?"

"Well, if I take close-ups, it'll look like your origami dinosaurs are life-size. You could make a book of them. Or just hang the pictures up in your room."

"Okay!" He gathers all the paper quickly, and

then he gently places each dinosaur in a decorated shoebox. "Let's go," he says.

Jayvee and I arrange his dinosaurs behind our property in the Gold Hills Nature Preserve. A couple of the fallen logs have prehistoric-looking fungi growing on them. The dinosaurs look great in this setting. The light is dappled, and I am getting some great shots. If Jayvee hadn't forgiven me already, I was sure he would when he saw these pictures.

"Jayvee, can you move that blue dinosaur a bit closer to the fiddlehead ferns?"

"Like this?" he asks.

"Exactly, and maybe bring the pink dinosaur closer to that mint green one?"

"That's a Pteranodon. It's supposed to fly. Want me to hold it in the air so it looks like it's flying?"

"No, that'll ruin the effect. I wonder if we can string it up and hang it from one of these bushes?" We could use fishing line," I suggest.

"You'd poke a hole in my dinosaur?" Jayvee asks.

"Just a little one. And if we used fishing line, it'd be hard to see it in the pictures. It would really look like it was flying."

"I don't want you poking holes in my dinosaurs. That's as bad as when you squished my

Dimetrodon." He scowls at me a little.

"Okay, we'll make do." I am about to suggest that we could perch and angle it on a log so it looks like it just touched down from flying, when through my viewfinder, I see something white and fluffy. Something that does not look as if it belongs in these woods.

"Jayvee," I whisper. "Try not to move much, but turn slowly, and tell me what kind of little animal is behind your right shoulder."

Jayvee's eyes grow wide, but he does as I ask. Growing up here, Jayvee is as used to animals as I am. So when he sees it, he quietly answers, "It's a bunny. Not a wild one, looking like that. Fluffy white with blue-blue eyes. It's gotta be someone's pet."

"Not again," I say. "We should rescue it, buddy. What do you say?"

Jayvee stays in crouched position and says, "I can probably get it if you go wide around me in case it gets scared and tries to run that way."

I do as he suggests. I circle wide, keeping an eye on the tiny thing. When I'm in position, I tell him, "Go ahead, Jayvee."

He moves slowly, and then—quickly. He swoops the bunny up before it even knew what was happening. Definitely not a wild rabbit.

"You have some fast hands there, my man," I say.

Jayvee beams. He holds the bunny firmly but gently. "Let's take it to Mom."

"Want me to gather your dinosaurs?" I ask.

"Be careful," he says. And I am.

Mom examines the bunny thoroughly. Jayvee and I prepare another cage in the critter barn for this new occupant.

"It's a female lionhead," Mom says. "Certainly not native. And I'd say only a little over eight weeks old."

"Lionhead?" Jayvee asks. "How do you know? It doesn't look like it has a lionhead."

"It will," Mom replies. "See this little ruff between its ears? As it gets older that ruff will extend right around its head. It'll look like a lion's mane. This will be a very cute rabbit."

Mom puts the bunny in the cage that Jayvee and I have prepared. She gives it a little pat on its head, closes the tiny door, and then sighs.

"What's wrong?" I ask. The bunny's water bottle is dripping a bit. I tap it.

"We are getting overrun by rabbits," Mom says.

"But they don't eat a lot," Jayvee says. "Do they?" He looks as if he thinks he's done something wrong.

"No, son, they don't. And I'm glad you found this little girl and were able to catch her. It's just that I thought we were going to have an easy post-Easter census. But it's climbing. One more animal means more work, and there's only so much time in a day."

"Do you need us to help out more?" I ask. I fiddle with the bunny's water bottle to make it stand up straight. The dripping slows. Then stops. Good.

"You kids have school." Mom rubs her forehead. "Sage is busier than usual with his classes this semester. We're all just spread a little thin right now."

"Oh," Jayvee says. "Do you wish I hadn't caught this bunny?" Jayvee does not look at Mom. He faces the bunny, but I can see his eyes glancing sideways.

"No, no, no," she says. "I am very happy you were able to rescue her. And we're fine here. We always manage."

Mom looks at me and smiles a funny smile: half smile, half frown. I shrug my shoulders and smile back at her.

Mom ruffles Jayvee's hair and pulls me into a hug. "I've raised such talented animal rescuers. Hey, I think I have a few oatmeal cookies left in the jar. What do you say we polish them off?"

Walking back to the house, Mom and Jayvee trade job title suggestions:

"Rabbit Wrangler."

"Bunny Buckaroo."

"Hare Herder . . ."

Meanwhile, I wonder how I can help Mom and our rehab center. There must be some way to get these bunnies adopted.

Chapter Five

. . . .

On Sunday, Maggie, Sunita, Jules, and I check on the ducklings as soon as we arrive. Maggie and Dr. Mac had already fed and cleaned up after them first thing this morning. The ducklings look better—and bigger—than they did just the day before. What a relief. We can't stop grinning at one another as we check their water bowl and adjust the heat lamp. Jules peeps sweetly to the healthy-looking ducklings before we move on.

We begin cleaning the exam rooms. They're right across the hall from each other, so we keep the doors open and talk with one another as we clean. Maggie and I work on the Dolittle Room, and Sunita and Jules handle the Herriot.

"It's strange having so few of us here today," Sunita calls from the other room.

Maggie is gloved and restocking supplies in the small cabinet beside me. She says, "I know David has been looking forward to the horse judging for months."

Sunita asks, "Is he a judge, or is Trickster being judged?"

Maggie closes the cupboard. "No, he and Josh are volunteer ambassadors. They're supposed to welcome people, get the judges coffee, run paperwork back and forth between the ring and the judges' booth. And something else. I can't actually remember everything he told me. Glorified gophers, Gran called them."

"How about Zoe?" comes Jules's voice from the Herriot Room.

"I don't know," Maggie begins. "She might have gone to the horse show. I haven't seen her since she walked across the street to David's house. If she did go, I'm sure she wasn't planning to muck stalls or do manual work of any kind, though. She was pretty dressed up."

That makes me smile. Zoe sure knows how to put an outfit together. She brings a lot of Hollywood glam to Ambler, Pennsylvania. But what could she be doing at the horse show? It doesn't seem like her kind of thing.

It's a quiet weekend at Dr. Mac's, which is unusual. But it means it's going to be a short day even without the boys' and Zoe's help. Sunita, Maggie, Jules, and I pet the cats for a while, then head out behind the clinic.

Dr. Mac has boarding kennels out back, where dogs that have recovered sufficiently stay until they're ready to go home. Plus, we board healthy dogs when their people are on vacation. But this weekend, Dr. Mac has only one dog—the recovering German shepherd, Baron—in the kennel. We take Baron out on the leash for a walk around the outside of the chain-link-fenced kennel runs. He is still wearing the cone around his head, and his legs are bandaged, but he gets around pretty well. He stops and sniffs at every weed, rock, and stick. He tries to get a big stick in the corner of the fencing, but his cone won't let him get close enough.

"Poor boy, do you want that stick?" Jules asks. Baron barks. He knows exactly what Jules is asking him. Jules tries to give the stick to him. But again, his cone makes it impossible for him to put it in his mouth.

"Try breaking it in half," Maggie suggests. You can always count on Maggie for solutions. Jules breaks the stick over her knee and gives the smaller half to the dog. Success. The shepherd carries it in his mouth for the rest of his walk.

When we get to the far side of the kennel runs, Baron drops his stick and barks like crazy. In the corner, where two of the chain-link fences come together, a rabbit is stuck.

"Oh no, get Baron out of here," Maggie urges Jules. Jules immediately pulls Baron's leash and trots back the way we came.

"I'll get gloves and a towel," Sunita says, running after them.

Maggie and I creep up and bend down to get a closer look at the rabbit. At first, it's hard to tell how it is stuck.

"Its back legs are tangled in the right corner of that fence, see? And I think its head is stuck in the bottom of the other fence," Maggie says, pointing to show me.

"I wonder how it managed to get stuck in both," I say. "Where was it going? What direction did it start from?"

"The big question now is how do we get it out of there without hurting it?" she asks.

The rabbit isn't bleeding. In fact, it doesn't actually look hurt, just stuck. But it's breathing fast and its eyes are wide and wild-looking.

"It's scared," I say. "It might bite."

"What if we untangle the back legs from the one fence first," Maggie suggests.

"O-kay," I say, unsure of how we're going to do this.

"Then we can put a towel over her head and pull her back through the other fence," Maggie says.

"Her ears might get caught if we pull her through backward," I say.

Maggie sighs, "I hate to pull her whole body through forward when it's only her head that's stuck." She sighs again. "But I see what you mean about her ears."

Sunita is back with gloves and towels. "Jules is locking Baron in his cage. She'll be back soon."

"Maybe we can bend the fencing up from the ground to make a really big hole, and then you can safely pull her backward," I suggest. "It looks—what's the word—pliable? I think two of us can bend and hold it while you get the rabbit out from beneath it."

We agree that we will try this. All of us put on the heavy work gloves that Sunita brought. Light, latex exam gloves would not protect us from a rabbit's razor-sharp front teeth.

Maggie drapes the rabbit in the towel and holds her firmly. I untangle the back legs from the first fence. Then Sunita and I get on opposite sides of Maggie and the rabbit. We pull the fencing toward us from the bottom as Maggie gently pushes the bunny's head down toward the ground. We don't want the bending fence to cut her. Bending the fence is harder than we thought it would be. Sunita grunts. I take a big breath. My biceps are killing me.

"Higher," Maggie whispers.

I look across to Sunita. She nods and we ease the fence up just a little more. Maggie slides the towel-wrapped rabbit back through the hole, and it's free. But then, Maggie lets go of the rabbit, and it races alongside the fence and then cuts toward the woods.

"You shouldn't have let it go!" I yell. "It could have spinal damage or other injuries!"

"I didn't mean to," Maggie says. "It twisted away from me. The towel bunched up, and she wriggled out!"

"Well, it couldn't have spinal injuries and run that fast," Sunita says. "I'm sure it will be okay." She's right. We did our best. We rescued the rabbit.

"We have a fence to fix," I say. "I'm pretty good at that." After we get pliers and a hammer, we fix the fence and go back to cleaning the exam rooms. What was supposed to be a quick walk with Baron to stretch all our legs turned into an hour's interruption and one rescued rabbit. Not bad for a potty break, I suppose.

All four of us are nearly done with the exam rooms. We just have to mop both rooms and then head to clean the recovery room. Dr. Mac is cleaning the operating room today, so we can skip it.

"We need a plan for the ducklings," I say to everyone.

Jules calls out from the Herriot Room, "I thought your family was taking them for now!"

"We are. But I mean something bigger. Something long-range."

"Like what?" Maggie asks.

Jules and Sunita stop what they were doing and stand in our doorway.

"Every year my parents complain about the post-Easter abandonments," I say.

"Gran, too," Maggie adds.

"So I've been thinking, we need to do something now. Not wait till next year."

Sunita steps into the Dolittle Room. "What can we do now?" she asks.

I look at my friends. "We need to find out who is selling these ducklings, chicks, and bunnies for Easter."

Maggie stops counting gauze squares and looks

up at me. "Good idea," she says. "But how?"

"We can divide it up and ask around. We've done this before. A couple of us can take the feed store. And the pet store. Jules, your folks aren't selling any animals at the hardware store, are they?"

"No. Why would you think that?"

"Some hardware stores do. I researched last night. Feed stores, tractor-supply stores, and hardware stores sometimes sell baby chicks to people who want to start a small flock of chickens. Some of those stores sell ducklings and bunnies at Easter, too."

Sunita's jaw drops. She closes it. "I had no idea," she says. "We need to get them to stop."

"But how?" Maggie asks. "People have the right to raise chickens if they want. Ducks, too."

"First, we can try to figure out who is selling them. Then we can tell the store owners what happens to many of these animals. Maybe we can get them to screen their customers. Find out who intends to actually raise the animals responsibly and who was thinking of a cute pet for a day. Or . . . well, I don't know. We'll think of something. But we do this this week, okay?" Sunita, Jules, and Maggie all nod.

Jules says, "Josh and I can check out the pet store. It's not far from us."

Sunita adds, "I'll join you. Maybe we should stop into the animal shelter and find out what they know. It might help us get a sense of how many abandoned pets we're all dealing with."

"Good idea. Maggie, do you want to go with me to the tractor supply and the feed store? We can get David to help. He has friends at both places, too."

"Sure. And Zoe, too. Right?" Maggie asks.

"Right," I say. "Zoe can charm them into telling us everything we want to know."

Sunita laughs.

"What if we did little presentations about this to our science classes?" I suggest.

"Oh, I don't know," Jules says. "It's hard doing that kind of thing in front of your whole class. And I wouldn't know what to say."

"We could write it together. Maybe make a poster. It wouldn't be like giving a speech. It would just be sharing a few facts with kids you already know." I'm feeling even stronger about this.

"Come on, Jules. What if we prepare something short as a group. We can each make a poster, and the presentation won't take long. Five minutes. Tops." I look at Sunita and Maggie. They don't look thrilled, but they shrug and nod yes.

"I'll post it on the blog, too," I add.

Jules still doesn't look convinced. "You like public speaking," she says to me. "You're good at it."

"I got good at it by doing it. You can do it, too, Jules. You can," I urge.

"But why do this with our classmates? They probably didn't buy any baby bunnies or ducklings," Jules asks.

"Education," I say. "If we can reach our classmates now, that's a whole lot of people who won't be so irresponsible in the future. Besides, they'll tell other people. It'll be a revolution!" I may be taking this a little far. But this seems to convince Jules.

She nods. Done.

"How about as soon as we're done cleaning, we make up a little sheet? Maybe ten bullet points, something simple? Then we can make copies for all of us and be ready for Monday." Everyone nods. Good.

"Wait until the rest of them hear what you've roped us all into, Brenna," Maggie says. "We should get back to work so we have time to work on the presentation."

We do just that. Working quickly, we finish cleaning the exam rooms. Jules brings the hot, soapy mop bucket to our door. "Want me to get your room? I'm in a mopping mood," she says.

Maggie laughs and waves Jules in. "Wouldn't want to crush your mood. Go for it."

That's when Zoe arrives.

"Where are the boys?" Maggie asks.

"How should I know?' Zoe answers.

"Weren't you with them at the horse show?"

"Why would I go to a horse show? I've been showing David's mom some new healthy recipes."

"You sure you weren't really there to flirt with David's older brother?" Maggie says.

"He needs to eat healthy, too, doesn't he?" Zoe says. She turns away from Maggie and winks at us.

We step into the hallway. Sunita leans against the doorframe. She says, "Brenna, tell us about the Outdoor Club meeting. Did you get many volunteers for the next stream cleanup day?"

I nod. "Nine. And they're solid volunteers. Even though their club is mostly for activities like hiking, kayaking, and camping, they also care about the environment."

"They go camping? Just students, no parents?" Maggie asks.

I shake my head. "They go with teachers. I met one of their advisers at the meeting. He's the biology teacher. And Mrs. Durant, my old Girl Scout leader, is another adviser. I think she teaches some kind of math at the high school."

"So girls and guys together, with no parents?" Zoe asks in a funny voice.

"With adult advisers," I remind her.

Zoe smiles and nods slowly.

Jules wheels the mop bucket out of the room. We step back to let her pass, and then we stand outside the Herriot Room watching her work. I guess we start to feel bad then because we all head to the recovery room to clean.

"You should see their meeting room," I continue. "Posters of their activities are everywhere. So many cool trips. In the summer they do a weeklong camping trip to the Adirondacks. They hike some of the high peaks—"

"You found out a lot about them. Did you do any talking during your presentation? Or were you just looking at posters?" Maggie teases. "And you know I still feel bad for bailing on you."

"Really, it was okay," I say. "And yes, I did do some talking. A lot of talking, as a matter of fact. They really liked my photos. And I know so much because I checked the group out online before my presentation. They have a great web page. I really want to join that club!"

"To show them your dead duckling picture?"

I hear Sunita say under her breath. I guess she's still mad about that.

"It sounds like they're not going to let you join," Zoe says.

Maggie hands me the sponges, and we start cleaning the dirty cages and sanitizing the clean ones. Maggie takes the high cages. Sunita begins in the corner by the ducklings.

"Well, they should. They should let all the Vet Volunteers join. We have the same interests, and we're mature. Most of us, anyway," I say. I'm on my knees, partially inside our biggest floor cage. "Middle school is so babyish compared to high school. You know, nobody fooled around while I was talking. It's like being with adults. They took me seriously. And then there's all the stuff we'll be able to do in high school. Do you know that some students study in another country for a semester or a *whole* year? And it seems like they all have jobs. How cool is that?"

Sunita answers, "We have jobs. Look at us here on a Sunday morning, cleaning and organizing."

"I mean *paying* jobs." I use my second sponge to wipe away the soapy water that has gathered in the corner.

"What? You think Gran should be paying us? We're Vet *Volunteers*." Zoe scowls.

"That's not what I mean. You know that's not what I mean. I love this. I love us. It's just that . . . it's that . . . I don't know." I stop scrubbing and sit back on my heels. "The high school students' lives just seem a whole lot more interesting than ours do."

"Well, the boys are cuter," Zoe says. She has her hand on her hip, as if she's ready for a photo shoot.

I'm not sure why, but Sunita looks a little mad at me. Maggie looks confused.

"Come on," I say. "Don't you wish you were in high school doing all sorts of interesting stuff? Don't you think we should join that club?"

Sunita walks over to Maggie and me. "Some day. But Brenna, why rush things? I love being a Vet Volunteer. And middle school is going well for all of us."

Maggie snorts. "Most of us, anyway."

Sunita continues, "We don't need to join a club for high schoolers. Why are you so dissatisfied with now?"

Dissatisfied? Is that what I am? No. I'm just ready for something new. They just don't see how great the older kids have it compared to us. I try to explain.

"Don't you ever feel like we're in this hold-ing place? I mean what is *middle school* anyway? It's all about what it's not. It isn't high school. It isn't elementary school. It's what? That school in the middle of the other two. A waiting place." I feel myself getting angry, and my voice getting too loud, and I don't exactly know why.

"Waiting place?" Maggie asks. "It doesn't seem like we do all that much waiting around. School seems like a lot of work. It's hard. All the time." She has finished her cage, so she closes its door. *Slam.* The clang causes the ducklings to loudly peep.

"Brenna, what do you wish was different at school?" Sunita peers at me—like if she looks hard enough, she'll understand how my brain works.

I take a breath and tell myself to calm down, speak slower, softer.

"It's not just school, I begin. "But, well, think about school for a second . . . we've basically been taking the same subjects since first grade. At the high school they have journalism, graphic design, photography! And the math and science classes. They'll be harder, sure." I glance at Maggie. She narrows her eyes.

"But much more interesting," I continue. "And you wouldn't believe all the clubs! I bet if we talked to the Outdoor Club's faculty adviser about the Vet Volunteers, they would make an exception for us. And you would like the kids themselves. The ones in the Outdoor Club, they don't fool around like David and Josh do. They don't throw things. They're too mature for that."

Sunita hands me a couple sanitizing wipes. "We will all get there. Soon enough."

"Not soon enough for me!" I'm too loud again.

"Whoa, what's going on?" Jules asks as she wheels in the mop bucket.

"Brenna wants us to get into some club that doesn't even want us. And nothing's good enough for her. School isn't even hard enough," Maggie says. "And I guess none of us is mature enough for her, either." Maggie pushes past me out into the hall. I hear the door between the clinic and her house slam.

"Ooh, she's mad," Zoe says, following her cousin.

"I just . . . I just . . . ," I try to explain.

"I didn't mean the Vet Volunteers weren't mature," I say to Jules and Sunita.

"Don't worry. They'll be back," Sunita says. Jules nods.

But that's the last we see of Maggie and Zoe for the day. Everything feels awkward, and none of us says much. Sunita, Jules, and I make up the short presentation. Sunita types it and prints out copies for each Vet Volunteer. We check on the ducklings once more and gather our things. Sunita leaves two copies on the desk for Zoe and Maggie. Jules takes one for Josh and one for dropping at David's on her way home.

As we step out the door, we almost trip on a package.

"Who delivers on Sunday?" Sunita asks.

People who abandon baby bunnies.

Chapter Six

· · · · · · · · · · · ·

The next day at school, I see all the Vet Volunteers at some point in the halls. Maggie sits in front of me in the same science class. She practically ignores me when I try to discuss us both going up after class and showing Mr. Shuler our possible presentation. So I go talk to him myself.

"Could I show you something I'd like to share with the class?" I ask Mr. Shuler. He's a good teacher and a friendly guy.

"What do you have there, Brenna?"

"I think this would take five minutes to present. And maybe a couple more for questions, if anybody had them." I show him the sheet with my outline. "I was going to make a poster to go with it. Maggie said she might help me with both."

Mr. Shuler looks up and back at Maggie still sitting at her desk.

"Something wrong between you two?" he asks.

"I'm sure she'll get over it," I say. But then I look back at Maggie. She glares at me. What is her problem?

"Well, you two have my permission. How about Wednesday? We should have some time right at the beginning of class."

"Great! Thanks," I say. I take my paper back from Mr. Shuler and turn to go back to my desk.

"If she doesn't 'get over it,' will you still do it?" he asks quietly. I look back.

"I'll do it. I don't have any problem doing it alone," I say. I pass Maggie's desk and see her frown as I go back to my own desk. Why is she so mad at me?

We don't all have the same lunch period, but David, Sunita, and Zoe are at our usual table. Sunita has her head buried in a book. She eats between page flips.

"I need to concentrate," she says to David when he tries to talk to her. So it's going to be one of those "tune-out" lunches with Sunita. Oh well. No hard feelings.

David talks to me between bites of his sandwich.

"Sunita told me about the bunny in a box," he says.

"Yep, another one abandoned. What is wrong with people?" I answer.

"We should do something about all these dumped animals," David says.

"This is exactly why we need to start by talking to the classes," I say.

David chews, Sunita reads, and Zoe stares off into space. I turn to look for Maggie, but she isn't in the food line, and I don't see her at any other table, either.

David stops chewing and says, "Ms. Ryan said it was okay to talk to the class. I'm gonna do it tomorrow. Can you make a poster for me?"

"David, can't you take care of it? I have to do my own," I say. I look over at Zoe. She avoids my eyes.

David takes another bite. "I guess. But it won't be as good as yours would be. Can I just draw a duck and color it in with a yellow marker?"

"Yes, but you could add more to it. Draw a chick and a bunny, maybe," I suggest.

"I don't think I can draw a chick," he says. "Maybe I can draw a rabbit. I'll try. You know, I could just borrow your poster. We're in different classes."

"Just make your own poster. Then we don't

have to worry about handing it back and forth," I say, annoyed.

David looks over at Zoe. He looks back at me and nods his head toward her with a puzzled look on his face. I shrug my shoulders.

"Zoe," I begin, "where's Maggie?"

"No idea," she says, and sighs heavily. "She might be avoiding you."

"Ah, come on," I say. "I know she's mad, but why exactly? And why aren't you as mad at me now as you were yesterday? I still don't know what that was about, either."

David looks at me as if I'm crazy. So I explain to him. "We had some trouble yesterday at the clinic."

David nods and chews. Sunita looks up from her book and frowns.

Zoe says, "I thought you were mad because Gran doesn't pay the Vet Volunteers. Maggie told me I misunderstood. So I'm not so mad anymore."

"Then what is Maggie so mad about?" I ask.

"I'm not getting in the middle of this," Zoe says. She takes a sip from her water bottle. "You'll have to talk to her." Zoe fixes me with a stern look.

"I was just talking about the club and high school kids. Maggie blew things out of proportion—"

"This is between you two," Zoe interrupts.

"Take it up with Maggie." Zoe gets up to leave.

Under his breath, David says, "Seems like a mad amount of mad going on."

I ignore him. And try talking to Zoe again.

"Are you going with me to the feed and tractor-supply stores this afternoon?" I ask her.

"I think I'll hang out with my cousin. She says she's not going anywhere with you today." Zoe stops a moment. "Listen, I don't want to be in a fight. Make up with her. This is too hard." She smiles a small smile, turns, and leaves.

Sunita looks up then back down at her book without saying a word.

David stops chewing. "I still don't know what that was all about. But I'll go with you. Want your oatmeal bar?"

I hand him my bar and an orange, too. Lunch period usually rushes by before you've had a chance to actually eat much. But today it drags. When the bell finally rings, I say good-bye to David and Sunita, and plow through the rest of the day.

After school, David and I walk to the feed store. My parents sometimes shop here, but a lot of their feed comes by mail order. When you're feeding foxes and baby porcupines, it can be hard to buy local, so it's been a few months since I've been in here. But I love it when I do come in. For one thing, it smells great. A little like oatmeal. A little like baby food—rice cereal with apple juice—and a lot like molasses.

"My dad is thinking of buying this place," David says. He sets a spinner of weird animal postcards spinning. It squeaks as it turns. I make it stop.

"Really? When?" I ask.

"Dunno. He's been talking to the owner about it. I might have forgot that I'm not supposed to say anything about it." David looks at me with a funny smile.

"I won't say anything to anyone," I reassure him.

We look around a bit. I don't see any animals at all. Maybe they don't sell them.

The store does sell things other than feed. I see stacks of salt licks for horses, cattle, sheep, and goats. And there's other stuff farmers use, like seeds and fertilizer. And one whole corner of the store is for poultry supplies. Waterers, egg baskets and cartons, heat lamps like we use in the clinic, and they sell chicken treats, too. That seems kind of funny to me for some reason. They also sell funky shade hats and weird lip balms and hand creams.

David shows me a tub of powder with a chimpanzee sporting a sore rear end called No-Monkey-Butt. He pulls out a couple dollars from his pocket.

"You're not thinking of buying that, are you?" I ask.

"Are you kidding?" he replies. I'm about to say "good" when he says, "How could I not buy something called No-Monkey-Butt? I can't wait to show Josh."

"And what will you use it for?" I ask.

"Laughs," David says.

The manager walks by, pretending he's not watching us. But he is, I can tell. David reads his package and chuckles to himself until I elbow him in the ribs. He looks up.

I flag down the manager and explain why we're there.

"Well, now," the manager begins. "We do sell plenty of baby chicks and ducks. And yes, bunnies. We sell them for a few weeks before Easter. But we sell them to adults, not to children such as your-selves. We are a responsible retailer."

I know that compared to this store manager, we are children, but it seems as if he's talking down to us. Why did he have to call us children instead of calling us kids? The manager starts to walk away.

"Excuse me," I say.

He turns around.

I continue, "We think it's the adults who are buying them irresponsibly," I say, trying not to sound annoyed. "They aren't thinking about caring for the animal for its whole life. They're just thinking about a holiday surprise."

"And that's not right," David adds.

"Now, now, I see what you're saying," the manager says, scratching the back of his neck. "But we sell to farmers as well as to folks looking for a pet. I can't be asking every customer what their intentions are."

"Their intentions?" David asks.

"What they plan to do with the animals. How they plan to care for them," the manager explains.

"Or how long they intend to keep them," I add.

"Exactly," the manager says. "I've heard of this being a problem in other areas of the country, but never here."

"But it is a problem here," I say. "We've had trouble for years at the wildlife rehab, and so has Dr. Mac. Finding homes for these animals is a springtime nightmare!"

"Well, I guess I'll have to stop by the clinic soon and talk to Dr. Mac and Gabe. We'll just have to set to thinking this through. Thanks, kids," he says, turns and walks away.

"That went great," David says, smiling.

"Really? Did you get the idea he only wants to work with adults? I feel a little brushed off," I say.

"Adults are always that way," David says. "Well, almost always. We're just used to being treated kinda like grown-ups at the clinic. And what difference does it make as long as he changes the way he sells them. Right?"

David is right. We made some progress.

"Off to the tractor-supply store," I say. But as we head down the far aisle to leave, we see a cage with two bunnies inside. One is dyed pink, the other, purple! There is a sign beneath the cage that shows the price marked down by five dollars.

"Wow," David says. "Those are so cool!"

"Are you kidding me? They must have dyed them. Real bunnies aren't colored pink and purple."

"They look real to me," David says. He peers into the cage.

"I know they're *alive*," I say. "What I mean is, that's not natural. It can't be good for them. We have to talk to that manager about this."

We walk to the nearby checkout counter and ask the lady at the register to page the manager for us.

"He just left," she says. "Won't be back from his break for an hour."

"I guess we can come back later," I say. "Let's go, David."

"Gotta buy this first," David says. He shakes that crazy powder and grins like a lunatic.

We walk to the tractor-supply store. It's less than a mile away and a couple streets off Old Mill Road. David reads his package aloud as we walk.

"Our fabulous product prevents terrible itching and soreness caused by friction.

"Used by motorcycle riders, farmers, truck drivers, horseback riders, and anyone else who suffers the indignity of rash."

David stops walking. "What is indignity, again? I used to know what it meant. I think."

"It means something that makes you feel embarrassed," I explain. "I can't imagine the way that you behave that you ever suffer the indignity of anything."

"Too cool, huh?" he says, walking again. "You know that I am."

"Cool isn't the word I would use," I say.

On the way, I think about those colored bunnies. Who will buy them? How long will they keep them? I think about what I should do about it.

We arrive at the tractor-supply store and walk around just like we did at the feed store. We don't see any sign of animals here, either. But there is an empty brooder in the middle of the floor. It still has wood shavings in it, but no chicks or duck-lings.

A lady sorting huge eyebolts in bins calls out to us from across the aisle, "They're all gone, kids. Sorry." She goes back to sorting.

We walk over to her.

"But you did have chicks, recently?" I ask.

"Yeah, well, the last of 'em went a couple weeks ago. We're not getting any more. Not till next year." She shakes the box in her hands into the larger bin and then plucks out a couple smaller eyebolts and puts them in another bin.

"Did you sell rabbits, too?" David asks her.

"Rabbits? Why would we sell rabbits?" she asks. She starts on a new box.

Neither of us knows what to say to that.

"Are you the manager?" I ask.

"Do I look like the manager?" she asks.

Again, we don't know what to say.

"Dieter Morris. Mr. Morris to you. He's the manager. Why?"

"Well," I begin, "we'd like to talk with him about abandoned chicks and ducks."

"And rabbits." David adds.

"I told you, we don't sell rabbits."

I shoot David a look. He's not listening, and

he's not helping, either. Instead, he's flipping his No-Monkey-Butt powder through his hands.

"Right, so about the abandoned animals, we'd like to talk to Mr. Morris about them."

The lady stops her sorting. "You kids oughta talk to the animal shelter if you're looking for abandoned animals. They got a lot of 'em. Dogs and cats, too. They once had a hedgehog. You ever seen a hedgehog?" she asks.

"We don't want to get any animals," David says and points to me. "She wants to talk to the manager so people will stop abandoning them."

"The manager ain't here now. But I think you kids should go over to the animal shelter. They'll help you out."

"Okay," I say. We aren't getting very far here anyway. I'll have to stop back another time when Mr. Morris is here.

"Be sure you pay for that on your way out if you're keeping it," she says to David.

"Oh, this is mine," he says. "I bought it at the feed store just a little while ago."

The lady looks suspicious.

"Really," David says. He fishes the receipt out of his pocket, but she doesn't even look at it.

"I didn't sell this to you. I would remember you." She points a finger at David.

"It's because I didn't buy it here. I told you, I bought it at the feed store." David tries to show her the receipt again.

"So why are you trying to return it here?" she asks, raising her chin and narrowing her eyes.

"I don't want to return it. I just bought it," he says. And then adds, louder, "At the feed store."

Well, okay," she says. "I was just being careful." She goes back to her work.

David and I leave quickly. "That was weird," he says.

It was. But at least we know where some of the animals are coming from. And even if we didn't get to ask if they screen the buyers, we know they sell chicks and ducks at the tractor supply and chicks, ducks, and rabbits—dyed ones, too—at the feed store.

I say good-bye to David and start toward home. If all went well for Sunita and Jules, they should have some information from the animal shelter and some from the pet store. We'll need to compile and figure out exactly what we should do with all this information.

That's all I can think about for now, because tomorrow afternoon, I meet with the Photography Club. It doesn't make sense to ask Maggie or Zoe to go, after all. Neither one is really speaking to me. Fine. It doesn't matter.

I think about how I need to reset my slide show, add a few new pictures, and put everything in the right order. That's going to take a lot of my time tonight.

In my mind, I swap one picture for another then swap it back. I think about the way the stores treated us today. They were nice enough. Helpful enough. But they treated us like little kids. I bet high school kids never get treated like that. That's just one more reason to look forward to leaving middle school behind.

Chapter Seven

. . . .

As soon as our school day is over, I walk across the parking lots to the high school. Their school day is over, too. The marching band is emptying out the main doors and assembling in an empty corner of the parking lot for practice. A couple buses are idling out front, waiting for some sports teams. It's loud and more crowded than the last time I came. I push through a bunch of students. I wonder if anyone can tell I'm from the middle school or if I look like a high school girl as I make my way through the halls.

I wasn't sure what to wear, so I changed my clothes a few times this morning. I could have asked Zoe for help, but it felt weird with Maggie still being mad at me. So I wore some new clothes my mom recently bought for me. All day long, I've been tripping on the hem of the pants and pulling the waistband up. Even the new shirt is a little too big. The sleeves are long, and the neck is too loose. It was awkward carrying my computer, camera, and portfolio across the parking lot while holding my pants up so they wouldn't drag in the puddles.

I'm hot and a little bit flustered when I get up to the second floor. I set my equipment down on the floor and double-check the room number on the closed door of the meeting room. Should I just walk in? Knock first? I decide to go in. Bad decision. There is some kind of after-school class going on. Everyone looks at me, and the teacher says, "Can I help you?"

"Sorry," I mumble, and slip back out the door. Now what? I look at my note once more:

Ambler High School Photography Club
Room 214. Tuesday. 3:10

The door says Room 214. It is Tuesday. I know it is. And now it's 3:20. This is making my stomach hurt. I stop a student walking by and show her my note.

"Photography Club. Oh yeah," she says. "They moved it."

"Do you know where they moved it to?"

"I'm not sure. During the afternoon announcements they said something about test prep going on in a couple rooms and the Photography and Key Clubs moving. I'm not in either of them, so I didn't pay attention. Sorry," she says, and starts to walk away.

"Wait," I call. "How can I find out where they've been moved to?"

She keeps walking but says over her shoulder, "Not sure. Probably posted on the activities bulletin board near the guidance office."

Well, that's just great. I'm going to be even later, and now I have to figure out where the guidance office is. A couple boys walk by, so I ask them.

"Downstairs where you pick up your schedule," one says.

"Across from the chorus room," his friend adds, and then shoves him into a wall as they both laugh and continue down the hall. Those two remind me of the boys in middle school. I guess they have a couple immature kids here, too.

I still don't know where that is, but at least I know to go back downstairs. I guess that the office must be somewhere close to the main entrance, but now that I've turned myself around, it isn't easy finding it. Eventually, I do.

On the bulletin board, three changes and cancellations are posted. I find:

TUESDAY 3:10 PHOTOGRAPHY CLUB ROOM 224

Seriously? Practically right where I'd come from. I race back upstairs. It's hard to move fast carrying all my stuff.

When I walk into the room, it's pretty noisy. Nobody notices me, and I'm not sure which one the leader, Najla, is. So I just go to the front of the room and put my computer down on the teacher's desk. The students are in small groups around the room. Some are looking at photos spread across tables. Others look over each other's shoulders—probably looking at digital pictures. A few kids in the corner laugh as one student salutes and pretends to fall down. What should I do?

I decide to set up. I turn on my computer and look around the room to try to figure out who's in charge. I wish there was a faculty adviser, at least. I'd know to ask the adult where and how to set up, anyway. My hands are shaking as I pull open my portfolio and spread it out. I wonder where the screen is? How can I project my photos without a screen to project them upon? For that matter, where is the projector? On the phone, Najla told me I didn't need to bring one, but I don't see one anywhere. This is a nightmare.

The group laughing in the corner finally spots me and comes over.

"Some people left because they thought you weren't coming," says a girl who might be Najla.

"I was told room two fourteen," I say.

"Yeah, they moved us without any notice," the girl says. None of the others seem particularly concerned. I guess they can't tell that I'm a little upset. I don't know if that's a good thing or a bad thing.

"Is this where you want me to set up?" I ask. My voice sounds funny. My stomach still hurts.

"Oh no. That's not good," the girl says. "The computer is back here. Give me your thumb drive, and I'll plug it in for you."

Thumb drive? I didn't bring a thumb drive. That's not what the Outdoor Club had me do for them. They told me to bring my computer, and I did. I take a moment to think this through.

"When I presented to the Outdoor Club last week, we just hooked my computer up to the projector. Can't we just do that again?" My stomach is doing little flips, and I might have to go to the bathroom, too.

"We don't have that kind of projector," the gesturing boy says. "This is a Smart Room. The projector is built into the computer back there, and your stuff will appear on the screen over here. It works great." He points to what I thought was a dry-erase board.

I bet it would work great—if they had told me to bring a thumb drive. And I guess I didn't have to haul my computer around all day at school and then over here. My eyes sting. I do not want to cry in front of everyone, but I feel embarrassed and mad. Why didn't anyone tell me anything?

I take a deep breath and say to the one girl, "Are you Najla?"

She nods, and I continue.

"So here's the problem. I didn't bring a thumb drive because you didn't tell me to. I don't know how I can do my presentation unless we can borrow the projector the Outdoor Club used. And I have to use the bathroom. Can someone tell me where it is?"

Najla eyes widen, and her mouth purses. "Well, I just assumed you would know. How should I know what the Outdoor Club uses? We do presentations all the time in Photography Club, and we always use the Smart system."

The boy looks at Najla, and I can tell he is as surprised by her tone of voice as I am. He says, "Wait a sec." He tilts his chin to the ceiling and furrows his brow. Then he says, "E-mail. Just e-mail your presentation to us, and we can run it through the system."

I breathe again. Since my computer is on and ready, I quickly e-mail my presentation file to the address he types in. As soon as he receives it on the school's computer, I head to the bathroom. I can't believe how clueless Najla is. First, she doesn't think to tell me that the room has been changed. Then she's mad that I'm late because of it. Plus she is irritated that I didn't assume I would need to bring different equipment. I guess not all high school kids are cool. I look at the time. I've already lost a half hour of presentation time. I'm going to have to cut it short. How?

When I get back from the bathroom, the faculty adviser is there. She and the students are sitting and looking at the screen. I glance at the screen, and instead of the first carefully selected presentation slide, it's a photo of the dead duckling. Oh no.

"Um, wrong file," I say to the helpful boy whose name I still don't know. I feel my face redden. What will they think of me? Sunita is a friend, and even she thinks I'm weird for taking it.

"Hold on!" a girl with a long skirt and giant earrings says. "That is an amazing shot. It tells a story."

"A sad story," I say. "The duckling had just died

because someone bought it and then abandoned it. We're pretty sure it was meant to be an Easter gift for a child. There was plastic grass in its throat when we found it."

"That's terrible!" she says.

"It really is," I agree. "Dr. Mac at the vet clinic tried to save it. But it was too fragile and dehydrated when we got to it."

"So sad," I hear a few people around the room say.

"We actually found four ducklings right here in the parking lot of the high school," I tell them.

"Oh yeah," a boy who seemed to be sleeping says. "I heard about that. Do you think somebody from here just dumped 'em?"

"Well, probably not a high school student," I suggest. "Most likely, a parent bought them for their kids, and when they saw how messy they were—and ducks are sooo messy—they decided to get rid of them. It's really terrible that whoever did this didn't at least find a place they could be cared for. The animal shelter, or Dr. Mac's clinic. This one didn't have to die."

Everyone is quiet for a moment. Have I said too much? The Outdoor Club was a lot easier to talk to. My stomach hurts, and I'm still way too hot.

"Still, it's a good shot," Najla says.

"Crazy good," a boy in the second row says. "What did you use to get that moody lighting?"

I look at the picture and try to remember. "A red-bulb heat lamp about four feet away and eighteen inches high off the surface gives it that apricot glow."

"Cool," he says. "I've never used a heat lamp bulb before."

I am about to tell him that I didn't set up the shot, that it was unintentional—almost a reflex—taking that photo. I am about to explain that the red bulb was a source of heat for the nearby healthy ducklings, but then my real first slide is projected, and I begin my wildlife photography talk.

I have to flip through quicker than I intended. But it's going okay. My stomach settles down, and I'm not wishing I had said no any longer. I wish they would crack a window, though.

We talk about wildlife. We talk about lighting. We talk about shutter speeds and specialty lenses. We talk about safety, and we talk about luck.

As the students ask questions, I flip to my last couple of slides. They're about the Environmental Club and Save Our Streams Cleanup Days. I have a sign-up sheet and handouts just like I did for the Outdoor Club, in case anyone wants to volunteer.

One girl—in head-to-toe black—asks me about joining the Environmental Club.

"We'd love to have some more members. My blog and e mail addresses are on the handout. You can get in touch with me."

"So this club," she continues. "Where do you meet? And is it a *middle school* club?" The way she says middle school sounds as if she meant kindergarten.

"We meet at the middle school. First Tuesday of the month. Four o'clock. And yeah, it's mostly middle school kids."

The girl looks less interested now. I see a couple kids pass their handouts back. So I quickly add, "But I'm pretty sure I'm moving the club to the high school soon."

The girl nods. "If you do, I'll think about it."

I should be happy about that. A couple other kids tell me they'll think about joining as they head out the door. I wonder if I've done the right thing suggesting it.

I've been thinking about it for a while—since last week anyway. After all, I did check out this school's auditorium and cafeteria in case we decide to move the meetings here. I know we'd get a lot more high school kids coming if the meetings were held here. And the Outdoor Club kids would see that the Vet Volunteers would be good members for their club. The Photography Club kids somehow made me feel too young, and I don't think any of them will join if the meetings are held back at the middle school. I'm sure of all this. So why do I dread telling the Vet Volunteers what I just suggested?

I look at the pile of handouts and my sign-up sheet. Nobody signed it. Only two handouts were taken.

I gather my stuff and walk downstairs. This time, everything looks bigger—and the remaining kids, not so friendly.

Chapter Eight

. . . .

Sage picks me up at the front entrance of the high school again. As we drive through the parking lot, I notice we both can't help but look in the direction of where we found the ducklings a week ago.

And that's when I see Nick and his girlfriend, from Outdoor Club, waving us down. Sage stops, and we roll down our windows.

"Hey, man"—Nick leans on the window frame and says to Sage—"I see you already fixed that muffler."

"Shop got me in fast," Sage says. "Hey," he says to Nick's girlfriend.

The girlfriend waves at each of us and then looks down at her phone as she quickly texts.

"Sorry I couldn't stop in to see your photog show," Nick begins. "I had to get some stuff done."

"It's okay," I say. Although I had really hoped to see him. One familiar face would have helped, especially at the beginning. Oh well.

"I was wondering about those baby ducks," Nick says. "They doing okay?"

Sage looks over at me to answer for both of us.

"The first three we all found are doing well," I begin. "But that fourth one you found didn't make it. It died a couple days later."

Nick looks seriously sad. "Jeez," he says.

His girlfriend looks up from her phone. "What's this?" she asks.

Nick answers, "One of the baby ducks didn't make it."

The girlfriend pats him on the arm, "Oh, I'm so sorry, sweetie."

"Did you guys ever find out who left them in the parking lot?" Nick asks.

Sage shakes his head. "We're on our way over to pick them up now, though," he says.

"We are?" I knew nothing of this.

Sage looks my way and says, "Yeah, Dr. Mac called Mom this morning and set it up. Says they're ready to be sprung."

"Cool," Nick says. "Glad they're going to your

place. Do you think you'll keep them?"

This time, Sage answers for both of us. "Naw. We're just a stop on the road to recovery. My parents work on releasing animals back to the wild or, if that isn't possible, finding them a permanent home."

"If we kept them all, we'd be overrun," I add. "Plus, they're meant to live in the wild."

Nick laughs. "Makes sense."

"Oh, also," I say, "I might be moving the Environmental Club meetings over here."

"Cool. I'm in," Nick says. He looks at his girlfriend and shrugs. "I think we both are. Keep me posted."

Sage taps the steering wheel. "We'd better get going to pick up those birds," he says. "You oughta come out to our place and take a look around. Visit the ducklings you helped save."

"Really?" Nick asks. "That'd be great. I bet I haven't been to the rehab center since my fourth-grade field trip."

Sage and I laugh because it seems like every fourth grader in the county passes through our place on a school field trip. Our dad even has a corny saying that he recites like a king might as the kids get back on their school buses: *"Go forth, Fourth Graders, and protect wildlife forever."*

Girlfriend looks up from her phone again, "What's this?" she asks.

"Nothing," Nick says as he waves good-bye.

We roll up our windows, and Sage drives out of the parking lot.

"How'd your thing go?" he asks when we're out on the main road.

"Fine. Well, eventually." I tell him all about the meeting room mix-up. Sage listens and nods and then says something that surprises me.

"Yeah, I can see that happening. High school kids can be a little self-absorbed." He shrugs. "I was like that. Do you remember?"

I think he is still self-absorbed sometimes, but he's giving me a ride so I'm not going to really answer that.

"I guess," is all I say. "How was school today?"

While we drive, Sage fills me in. It's been pretty hard for me to imagine how a college day actually goes. I know they don't have bells to tell them when class is over. And he sometimes has long stretches between one class and another, and he can do anything he wants during that time. Sage tells me he usually either studies or eats. There is a dining hall instead of a cafeteria, and you can just go there whenever you have time to eat. I guess it's like a restaurant. I know he likes college.

High school will be a little like college, I guess.

"So Sage, what do you think about me moving the Environmental Club meeting? Do you think anybody will be mad if I do?"

"Why would anyone be mad?" he asks.

Exactly. Why would anyone be mad? Well, I guess I know who might be. But why *should* anyone be mad? It's just a building switch. No big deal.

I guess I am not paying attention as we drive because all of a sudden we are in front of Dr. Mac's clinic.

"We have to be quick," he says. "I've got lots to do at home."

I grab the crate from the backseat, and we walk into the clinic. Zoe meets us as soon as we walk in.

"Hi, Sage," she says, all flirty.

"How ya doing, Zoe?" Sage says, crossing his arms in front of him. He smiles at her, which makes her smile even bigger. He glances at me, and I can tell he's amused.

"Just great," Zoe says. "I was wondering if you could help me move a bookcase in the living room?"

"Can't you wait for Dr. Mac to help you move it?" I ask.

"Gran is working on a cat right now," Zoe says. Then, turning to Sage she asks, "So could you?"

"I guess, if we can be quick," Sage replies. "You can help, too," Sage says to me, uncrossing his arms.

"Gran needs her help. Come on," Zoe says, leading Sage through the clinic to the house.

Maggie comes through the house door and Zoe squeezes by her. Maggie looks back over her shoulder as Sage and Zoe go into the house.

"What's that about?" she asks. Maggie is almost friendly. Maybe all is forgiven.

"Zoe wants help moving a bookcase," I reply.

"This minute? She's been talking about that bookcase for weeks. She keeps rearranging the living room only to put it back the way it was." Maggie laughs. "She'll probably make him try one of those kale shakes she keeps trying to give me."

"Sage might actually like that," I say. "But I have the feeling that Zoe is just trying to get his attention."

"That's Zoe," Maggie says.

We look at each other in silence for what seems like forever. I want to say I'm sorry, but I'm still not sure what I ought to be sorry for.

"So," Maggie begins, "Zoe and Gran think I might have overreacted to what you said about wanting to be in high school. I guess they're right."

"You realize we'll be in high school *together*, right?" I say.

"Yeah, but high school is going to be hard. At least it will be for me," Maggie says. "I'm not in any hurry to get there."

"They have after-school help there, just like at our school. I know, because Sage stayed after *a lot* for Spanish," I say. "And you know I'll help you when I can."

Maggie smiles. "Okay, but I'm still not going to weasel my way into that Outdoor Club with you. Let's not rush things, okay?"

I'm just going to have to work on getting into the Outdoor Club myself. Oh well. At least Maggie and I have made up. I feel lighter. And then, I decide to tell her what I said to the Photography Club students. Just to clear the air.

"One more thing, I might have told the Photography Club kids that we're thinking about moving the Environmental Club meetings to the high school," I say, as fast as I can.

"You *might* have told them?" she asks.

"I did tell them."

Maggie doesn't say anything. At first. Then, "What?! Why? I can't believe it." Maggie is angrier than I've ever seen her. "You're not in charge of everything, you know. It's not your decision."

Before I can answer she storms away. Again.

Sage is beside me. "What was that about?"

"I might've messed up," I say quietly. Sage pats me on the shoulder. I swallow hard. We go find Dr. Mac.

"You're here," Sunita says, and waves us back to the recovery room, where Dr. Mac is working on a shiny-coated silvery black cat. I can tell by the way she's handling it that the cat is sedated so it doesn't feel any pain.

Sage whistles. "Good lookin' cat."

"Hi, Sage, Brenna," Dr. Mac says. "Yes, he is. His owners named him Seal. Looks appropriate, don't you think?" Dr. Mac finishes wrapping a bandage around the cat's left hind leg. "However, this little guy seems much more interested in the road than in the water. This is the second time in three years that I've had to set a broken bone. He likes to race cars. Ever heard of a cat like that?"

"No," I say, "though David's cat likes to play fetch. Need any help?"

"I'm good. I'll be with you two in just a moment." Dr. Mac finishes by giving the cat a shot and putting him into one of the high cages. She scrunches his blanket up beneath his head. Lots of cats like to rest like that. Seal closes his eyes.

Dr. Mac removes her gloves and washes her hands.

"I've given your mom all the care info I have. I trust that your family knows a lot more about taking care of ducks than I do. So I know they're in good hands."

I put the crate on the stainless steel table and open the door.

"All set," I say.

Dr. Mac picks up two ducklings and motions Sage to pick up the third. The ducklings look so small in the crate. Their bodies are nothing but dandelion-yellow fluff with marigold-yellow bills and webbed feet. Their feet almost look too big for their little bodies. They stumble over one another, perhaps looking for the heat lamp. They are peeping up a storm, even the one we worried was too quiet before. I close the crate door when all three are inside.

"Here is a bag of the food I've been giving them. It's from Ambler Feed, if you want to get more. Or, of course, taper and mix in if you're going to change their feed." Dr. Mac hands the bag to Sage.

"Ducks are pretty resilient to feed changes," Sage says. "I'm sure they'll be fine, whichever way we go."

Sage takes the crate with him. Sunita waves good-bye.

In the parking lot, I can hear the hard *slap, slap, slap* of Maggie's basketball as she dribbles. Even though I can't see her from this spot, I can tell by the sound that she isn't taking any shots at the basket. Just dribbling. *Slap, slap, slap.*

Chapter Nine

· · · · · · · · · · · ·

Mom and Jayvee are in the critter barn when we pull up. They already have the heat lamp on and a bowl of feed set up in the stock tank. Sage and I set the ducklings onto the wood shavings, and Mom slips the waterer in. They drink right away. Dip, lift, swallow.

"I love ducks!" Jayvee says. "I love their cute mouths."

"Bills, sweetie," Mom says. "They have bills."

Jayvee is right—those bills are adorable. I get my camera out of Sage's car. I might as well get some shots of them on their first day with us. As I walk back into the critter barn, everyone else is coming out.

"Can you take over the evening feed and clean, Brenna?" Mom asks. "I have to get your brother to his school's open house. Dad is meeting us there. And Sage has plans. You okay with all this?" Mom spreads her arms toward the open barn door.

"Got it. No problem," I say. Mom pats my shoulder.

"You're a sweetie," she says. Then she leans in close and whispers, "We'll probably take Jayvee out for ice cream after. So we might be a little late."

Poe jumps on my shoulder as soon as I walk back in.

"How you doing, boy?" He nibbles at my ear, and I know he is just fine. But then again, I've been ignoring him a bit lately. Poor fella. I really should spend more time with him. Soon.

Poe stays on my shoulder as I get down to business, refilling bunny hayracks and checking water bottles. I clean droppings out and cuddle each bunny. They eye Poe, but none of them tries to jump out of my arms.

I feed three orphaned turkey chicks. I move around the barn and check on the snapping turtle, very carefully. I add some greens to his box and move on.

The ducklings are lying down cuddled up beside one another. They are inches away from their waterer. I bet ducks always like to be near water. They aren't peeping at all. Are they okay? I don't think I've ever heard them completely quiet. I bend down a little to see them better— Poe adjusts his balance on my shoulder. The heat lamp's glow shows me that they are all fine, closed eyes, all asleep. I keep the flash off to let them doze and snap a picture of them. This was probably a tough day for them, too. Changes are always hard for animals. And for people.

Maybe that's what Maggie and Zoe are worried about. Changes. But we're not changing schools, yet. We all still do Vet Volunteers together. I just think we can do some new things with some new, older people, too.

I place Poe back on his perch. I make one last check of the cages and containers. This barn is getting overcrowded. It's too bad that most people have no idea how many innocent animals are abandoned. I wish I could think of something to make my parents' job easier. I wish I could think of more than just posters and presentations to help.

I leave Poe in the barn and go outside to check the fox enclosure. This is usually a busy playtime for them. From my regular spot, I can't see any of them. They must all be inside the den. I turn toward the house when I catch a flash of copper out of the corner of my eye. I creep toward the fox enclosure.

Oh no! A fox kit is squirming his way out through the fencing. I run toward it, wishing I had my gloves and some help. But if I don't get to him quickly, he'll be out of there and who knows where.

How is he doing this? And then I see it. Oh no. He has opened up one of my fence patches. I must not have done a good job of repairing it. How will I push him back through and into the enclosure? As I get closer he sees me. He wriggles backward, falls on his behind, and runs to the coop. Whew. That was lucky for me. It would have been terrible if he had gotten out. I run back to the critter barn for gloves, flashlight, and needle-nose pliers. This time, I'll patch it right.

As I kneel in front of the fence, it occurs to me that this kit might not be the only one escaping. Even though we try not to let them ever see us, I have to break that rule. I need to check and count the kits. I move to the front of the coop, crouch down low, and shine my flashlight into the open-front coop. Three sets of fox eyes glow in the dark of the small coop. Three. That means one is missing.

My heart beats fast. How will I find a fox kit

now? It's getting dark. I scan the yard. Where could he have gone?

It's hard to think clearly when I'm imagining how much trouble I'm going to get into for not patching the fence right. And what danger this baby could be in. I take a moment to think. A fox is going to be most comfortable on the edges of forest. Well, that is when they're not staying close to their mothers. So I should probably look over there first. The woods are only ten feet away from this spot. But how will I catch an escaped kit?

Strawberries. Mom said they have loved the strawberry treats she has placed in the enclosure. Okay, I'll get strawberries. But how will I actually catch him? I wish my parents were here. Or some of my Vet Volunteer friends. Or Dr. Mac or Dr. Gabe. I don't think I have time to call and wait for anyone to get here. And I'm not sure how much my Vet Volunteer friends want to help me right now.

Think, Brenna, think. The raccoon trap! We have a humane trap that my parents have used to catch injured raccoons and skunks safely. I know that foxes are harder to trap, but maybe a kit will be fooled into going into it.

We keep the traps inside my dad's workshop. I've watched my parents set them dozens of times.

I take two traps and a handful of strawberries to the edge of the woods. It seems like a long time ago that I photographed Jayvee's origami dinosaurs here.

The traps are the size of a small cat carrier. I set them up about five feet apart on the wood's edge. I place the strawberries on the inside plate. Once the kit gets far enough in, he'll trip the wire that closes the door behind him.

My camera is still around my neck. It would be great to get an action shot of the kit going into the trap. But I don't dare, in case it scares the fox away. And that's if everything works out perfectly. I'm starting to doubt the chances of that. But what else can I do?

I move away from the traps, about twenty feet. I crouch in the shadows of my dad's workshop and stay still. I stay there a long time. My calves are tingling and my thighs and ankles hurt. It's getting so dark that I can't quite see the traps.

I'm not sure what time it is. But I must have been here about an hour, and I'm thinking that I may need a Plan B. I'm afraid that Plan B probably means phoning my parents. We're supposed to be caring for these animals, and I've put one in danger. All sorts of terrible things can happen to this baby overnight. My parents will be furious with me. They'll be disappointed. They might not think I'm mature enough to stay by myself or care for animals unsupervised.

Then I hear a snap! I spring up and rush toward the trap. I won't have to tell my parents after all. And then I hear another snap! Have I miscounted? Did two fox kits escape? I slow down and approach quietly. I let my flashlight beam sweep over the first trap. It's the fox kit! I am so relieved.

But then, what's in the other trap? I take a couple steps toward it and sweep the beam across the second trap. Uh-oh. It's a skunk. I've caught a skunk. What are the chances that I would catch one animal, let alone two, only moments apart? Now what? Things just keep getting worse.

The kit is between the skunk and me. If the skunk sees me and sprays, he'll get the kit, too. I think about approaching from another angle. Maybe I should go into the woods and come out right behind the fox trap. Still, the skunk might see me and get scared. A scared skunk sprays. But if I get down on my hands and knees and crawl up to the trap, I might be able to grab the trap without the skunk seeing me. This would mean crawling through the woods. Crawling over roots and rocks and logs quietly. That's going to hurt.

But I have to do it. I sweep out past my dad's

workshop, hoping that the skunk hasn't noticed me. Then I creep through the woods until I think I'm directly behind the fox trap and still far enough away from the skunk. I drop down onto my hands and knees and crawl as quietly as I can. I stop every once in a while and listen. The roots and rocks jab my knees. It's a good thing I have gloves on because all of these twigs would hurt more than they already do. My face breaks an invisible spiderweb as I crawl on through. I hope the spider isn't in my hair. I brush the webs away from my mouth and keep crawling.

I am just about to the trap when I see something white to my left. I stay still and look. Oh no, it's another skunk. No, it's three or four skunks. Babies. I cannot believe this. I must have trapped their mother. I have separated a mother from her babies. That's not good. Now what?

My heart is beating fast. I worry that my breathing is too loud and too fast. Can baby skunks spray? I have no idea. Okay, one thing at a time. I have to chance it. Crawling a little farther, I grab the handle on top of the trap and pull it toward me. The skunk babies stay still. The fox kit looks at me with big, shining eyes. I'm sure I am scaring it, but I have no choice. I crawl backward with the cage—a hard thing to do—until I think I'm safe to stand. Then I hold the cage away from me because I don't know if the fox will scratch or bite me through the cage. Even though I would totally deserve it.

I make a wide circle past the workshop, coming out on the far side of it. I can approach the fox enclosure without the mama skunk seeing me, I think. Quickly, I open the door of the enclosure fence and set the trap down just inside. I hope the fox mother isn't healed enough to charge at me to get to her baby. I fumble with the clasp, trying to release the kit. The mother stays back in the coop, but she barks at me. The kit is silent. Finally, the clasp comes loose and the kit races out the trapdoor toward his mother. I pull the trap back and slam the enclosure door shut.

Okay, one problem solved. The kit is back. I repair the fence. Now I just have to somehow let the skunk out so her babies don't get lost or starve overnight, and I'll be all set. How do I do that without getting sprayed? If I can figure this out, my parents don't need to know how I messed up.

But just as I'm turning around, the headlights from my parents' car sweep over me. Darn. Now I have no choice but to tell. I slowly walk over to meet my family.

Mom sends Jayvee inside, and I try to explain to

my parents what is going on. I show them the hole that I cut and patched.

"So the kit is back with its mother?" Dad asks.

"And you've trapped a mother skunk," Mom says in a stern voice.

"That's about right," I say.

I follow Mom into the house while Dad masks and suits up to release the skunk. He has plenty of experience, but it's not a sure thing that he can release the skunk without getting sprayed.

"Have a seat," Mom says when we get to the kitchen. I sit.

"Mom—" I begin, but my mom holds her hand up for me to stop talking.

"So you cut a hole without asking first," Mom says. She leans against the kitchen counter, her arms crossed in front of her. "And you did this in order to take pictures. And then you patched the fence." She pushes away from the counter and takes a step toward me. She keeps her arms crossed.

She continues, "And it didn't occur to you that you might need permission from us?"

"I thought if I patched it right, it wouldn't be a problem," I say, looking down at my hands. I shift in my chair and try to sit straighter.

"And . . ." Mom prompts.

"And . . . and, I guess I figured if I asked, you

would say no," I whisper. I hadn't thought out my reasons until I said that. Bad excuse.

"Brenna," Mom drops her arms and then raises them up to her head. "I might have expected this when you were younger, but not now."

"I'm really sorry about the fencing," I say.

"I thought you were more mature than this," Mom says, sitting down beside me.

More mature? I thought I was, too. My stomach does a little flip.

"I'm sorry," I say again. What else can I say? I really messed up.

"Your father and I will talk about an appropriate punishment. Head up and get ready for bed," Mom says. She taps the table and sighs.

"My science class presentation is tomorrow. I still have some work to do on it."

Mom shakes her head slowly and says, "Fine. Don't stay up too late."

I listen for Dad to come in. I can tell he didn't get sprayed because we would already smell it if he did. Whew. That's one more relief tonight. I turn on the computer.

Mom pokes her head in a little later.

"Your father says he's going to show you how to properly make holes and patch that fence. He seems to understand your need to take pictures clear of the fencing. You better pay sharp attention so that this never happens again."

"I will, I promise." I give my mother a big hug.

"This doesn't mean there won't be punishment for your poor judgment, because there will be." But she hugs me tight and pats my back and says, "Next time, do better."

I don't know yet what the punishment will be. But it's good to know I'm already forgiven. I go back to my project.

Maggie and I never did talk about doing it together. I can't imagine she wants to work with me now. And it's too late to call her anyway. I have to research and make a poster. Now I wish I hadn't told David that we each had to make our own. I would have liked to borrow his and save myself a little work tonight.

I research and work on my presentation for hours.

I don't mean to. But when I get involved in animal research, it's hard to know when to stop.

Besides people buying and then abandoning chicks, ducklings, and bunnies, I find out how they dye them. It's crazy! Some people inject the chick eggs with dye a couple days before they hatch. And other people mist on a spray paint when they're just hours old. The people who do it say it's non-toxic and doesn't hurt the animal. But that's ridiculous. It just adds to the idea that the animals are for decoration. If people want bright and pastel colors at Easter, they should dye Easter eggs, buy jelly beans, eat marshmallow chicks. Not turn living creatures into toys.

I think about the dyed bunnies at the feed store. I think I know what I will do about them.

I finish my report. When I am done writing it, I print out some photos of dyed bunnies and chicks and attach them to my poster board. I think about bringing in my computer to show a few photos that I took of our ducklings but then decide I have enough without it. I stack my report and poster beside my bed and look at the clock. It's after three in the morning! If my parents knew I was still up, I'd be in so much trouble. More trouble than I'm already in, anyway.

The next morning, Maggie is still ignoring me when I get to science class. I walk past her and bring my report and poster up to show Mr. Shuler.

"Oh Brenna, we agreed on a short report. By the look of that stack of paper, you would need the whole period. I'm afraid I can't give you that much time." He shakes his head slowly.

"I'm sorry. I guess I got carried away," I say holding my stack.

"What can we do here?" Mr. Shuler asks. He

picks up my poster and reads it. "This is good work, Brenna. As usual. But you're going to have to present the class with an edited version. Ten minutes. Tops," he says.

I leaf through my papers and think about what to say and what to leave out. Mr. Shuler passes me a highlighter, and I try to work quickly while he tells the class about the upcoming robotics competition.

I decide to talk about how fragile ducklings are and their need for water. About how they would most likely drown if abandoned. How many bunnies are bought as pets and then let go in the wild where they are not capable of surviving. And finally, about the crazy practice of dyeing and buying colored chicks and bunnies.

The whole class is interested in my report. Even Maggie, as much as she tries to hide it, is paying attention. And when I am done, my class claps. This is a surprise because it isn't the polite kind of clapping that kids do when a teacher claps. It's spontaneous. I bet they care as much as the Vet Volunteers do about the terrible things happening to all these baby animals.

"Well done, Brenna," Mr. Shuler says. He stands and leans on his desk.

"Thank you. Is there a way to share these reports at the high school? David Hutchinson, Sunita Patel, and Zoe Hopkins have posters, too. And maybe Maggie." I look back at her desk. I can tell she heard me say her name, but she isn't looking my way. "Maybe we could present in some biology classes?"

"Interesting thought," Mr. Shuler begins. "Let me see what I can do. I'll get in touch with the department head over there."

And then I have another idea.

I will explain my idea to everyone at lunch.

But when I get there, Maggie—again—is a no-show. She's avoiding me, I'm sure. She's putting so much effort into it. And as ticked off as I am about it, I'm also worried that she might not be eating lunch just to be sure she doesn't have to talk to me.

Sunita has her book with her again. She nods as I sit down and immediately goes back to reading. She fishes celery sticks out of a plastic baggie without looking and nibbles away.

David eats and talks to his buddy, Bruce, who sits directly behind him. Bruce's table is always a little bit wild and a lot too loud for the size of the cafeteria. And the fact that David sits right behind him doesn't stop Bruce from yelling over to our table. Bruce is also in Maggie's and my science class.

"Did you see Brenna's report?" Bruce shouts to David.

David tips back on his chair's back legs so he is face-to-face with Bruce.

"Nope. Bet it was good, though," he says. That's one of the great things about David. He isn't embarrassed to sit with girls in the cafeteria. He doesn't pretend not to like any of us Vet Volunteers whenever he's with his school friends. He treats us the same slightly crazy way, no matter where he is or who he is with. David is true David.

Bruce says, "It was." And then yells, "Hey, Brenna, the part about the chick dyeing was awesome!"

I am sitting in front of David, so there is no reason for Bruce to yell at me. But Bruce is Bruce.

"Glad you liked it," I say in a regular voice. I always hope Bruce notices that he can hear us just fine, but he never takes the hint.

Then David tips forward so all four legs are on the floor. His brow is furrowed, and he actually stops eating. "Did we have some chicks die, too? I thought it was just the duckling."

"Bruce is talking about dyeing. With a y," I say. "Not dying with an i. Wait a second. I guess that's dyeing with an e not dying with an i. You know, like the bunnies at the feed store?"

Zoe and Maggie have joined us. Maggie doesn't look at me, but just coming to the table is a great start.

Zoe sits and asks, "What's this about dying?"

She shakes her head and opens her lunch sack. David looks even more confused.

I try again. "You know how people tie-dye shirts and pillowcase? And some people dye their hair?"

Zoe nods.

"Well, there are people who actually dye—as in color—animals. Specifically, baby chicks, ducklings, and bunnies. I talked about it in my science class report," I tell them.

Zoe snaps the salad bowl closed. "You have got to be kidding!" she says. "Is that legal?"

"Some places it's not. But too many places it is. In fact, David and I saw two dyed bunnies at the Ambler feed store."

"It's true," David says. "Pink and purple."

I take a spoonful of yogurt. I won't tell the Vet Volunteers what I intend to do about those bunnies. They just wouldn't understand. But I need their help with the second part of the plan.

"There is something we can do about it."

"What's that?" David asks. He swipes my banana. "May I?" he asks, holding it up.

"Go ahead," I say. "Anyway, I talked to Mr. Shuler about us bringing our reports to some of the high school science classes. Not all of them, maybe just the biology classes."

David looks at Zoe.

Maggie says, "Would you stop trying to make us go to the high school?" She wipes her mouth with her napkin. "None of us want to go with you."

Maggie looks over at David, as if daring him to contradict her.

David looks at me and shrugs his shoulders. He tips back on his chair and asks Bruce if he has any food to spare.

Zoe says, "I wouldn't mind going over to the high school." She grins. "If it will help animals."

Maggie stares at her cousin and says, "Sunita isn't going to want to do this, either."

Um, Sunita is sitting right there.

"Sunita can decide for herself," I retort.

This gets Sunita out of her book. She looks up and glances around at us without understanding.

I take a deep breath. It makes no sense to get worked up about any of this. If my friends knew some high school kids, they would not be fighting me on this. So I try to explain.

"Listen, there is nothing to worry about. Nothing for any of us to be nervous about. Why is everyone so anxious about the high school? They're just students. Like us."

No one says anything. Maybe they don't understand.

So I explain, "The high school kids can get more done. People listen to them more than they listen to us." I turn to David, "Remember when we were at the feed store and the tractor-supply store?"

He nods.

"Well, they would have taken us more seriously if we were older. If we had some teenagers helping us with our Vet Volunteer projects—like this problem of abandoned animals—we could get so much more done. For instance, Nick, one of my friends in the Outdoor Club, I bet he would want to help us. And I'm thinking of moving our Environmental Club meetings to the high school. They have bigger rooms, and I know we'd get more high school kids participating if we held the meetings there."

I look over at David. He isn't saying anything for or against. Sunita looks stunned. Maggie looks down at her sandwich. Zoe is quiet, too.

That's when Mr. Shuler stops by our table. "Hi, kids. Brenna, I got the okay for those reports. We'll talk later about sending you kids over."

Mr. Shuler leaves, and Sunita says, "I don't

understand all of this high school interest."

Maggie says, "Brenna prefers the company of older kids. She's choosing them over us."

"Yeah," Zoe adds, "she's abandoning all of us."

I don't feel like seeing my friends after school, so I decide to go to the Outdoor Club's meeting. I probably shouldn't be going there uninvited, but I'm sure if I can just talk to the faculty adviser, they'll let me stay. Nick probably doesn't know that it's okay because no one from the middle school ever wanted to join before. But it's a club, not a class, so how could they have rules against middle school students?

I scoot up to the room where they hold their meetings. But there's a sign on the door reminding the club members that the bus for the Envirothon will be out front at 2:30. Rats, they're on a field trip. I'll go sit in on the Photography Club meeting, as long as I'm here. Maybe that adviser can tell me how to go about joining a high school club.

I slip into the classroom and take a seat by the door. Everyone stares. The whole room goes quiet. The adviser crosses the floor and says, "Brenna, right? What are you doing here today?"

Before I can answer, I hear a student in the back say, "Are we babysitting today?"

Another girl says, "Hope we're not expected to change diapers."

My face goes red. I can feel it burning. The adviser walks me out and says, "Did you leave something behind?"

"I just thought that maybe it would be okay—"

"We can't have students who aren't enrolled here just roaming around the school. You were invited yesterday. But you may not just barge in anytime you want. I'm so sorry, but it's against the rules. We'll see you again when you're in high school, dear."

She says all this with a smile on her face. But her eyes are not smiling. What's worse, she left the door open so all the kids heard her chew me out. I don't think I've ever been so embarrassed in my life. As I leave, I hear a boy shout out, "Busted."

On the school steps, I turn the opposite way from home and start jogging. I am going to do something grown-up right now. I am going to do something that I can tell the Outdoor Club about. They're nicer than the Photography Club kids, anyway. They'll be impressed. I bet I'll be invited to join when they hear what I've done.

I rush into the feed store and quickly walk down the aisle toward the cage with the dyed bunnies. As I'm looking at the latch, I hear a familiar voice, "Hey, Brenna, can't stay away, huh?"

It's David. And I see David's father behind him talking to the manager. Rats. David looks at my face and says, "What's up? What are you doing?"

"I'm going to free these bunnies," I whisper. Somehow saying it out loud—even whispering— makes this now seem like a bad plan.

"Free them to where?" David whispers back.

"The rehab center," I reply.

"And then what?" he asks.

"I don't know. Find them homes when we find homes for the others? I haven't really figured that part out." I feel ridiculous all of a sudden.

"But that's stealing, isn't it?" David stares at me. He looks disappointed with me.

"I don't really think it's stealing if we give them a better life," I reply.

"I think it's still stealing, and how do you know they'll have a better life than with whoever it is already bought them?" He points to a SOLD sticker attached to the sign. When David makes more sense than I do, it's time to go home.

I let out a big sigh, and as the air rushes out of me, so does all thought of this ever having been a good idea.

"Please don't tell anybody what I was about to do," I say to David.

"Our secret," he replies. "Come on, my dad will drive you home. We're leaving in just a sec."

I try not to look at the store manager's face as I wait for them to finish their conversation. Even though he doesn't know what I was going to do, I wonder if he can feel my shame, anyway.

Chapter Ten

. . . .

At home that afternoon, I spend time with the ducklings, the bunnies, and Poe. My crow usually makes me feel better when things feel wrong. He is such a good listener.

"Maggie and Zoe think I'm abandoning the Vet Volunteers for the high school kids. I almost stole some bunnies, and the high school kids don't even want me." My chest feels heavy. If I think about this too much, I'll cry. I give Poe a sunflower seed from my pocket. He nibbles his special treat and pushes his head up under my hand to see if there might be more. I pull another seed out of my pocket for him. I munch a couple, too.

"I'm not a thief. And you don't think I've abandoned anyone, do you, my friend? No. No, you don't. Because how is including new friends abandoning old ones? I was just trying to bring everybody together. That's all. But it looks like I'm not exactly making new high school friends, after all, am I?"

Poc looks at me and cocks his head to the right. Is he disagreeing with me?

"Middle school can be so lame, can't it, Poe?"

Poe hops away. I'm not sure that I'm winning him over.

It's time to take care of the ducklings. I shovel out some of the messy wood shavings from the ducklings' stock tank. They run away from my shovel, peeping. As soon as I put new wood shavings down, all three waddle over to that side.

"Nice and clean, right?" I say to the fluffy yellow babies. Immediately, one poops. "Okay, we were clean for a couple seconds anyway."

I place Poe back on his perch and feed him a few more seeds. I take a few quick pictures of him. Poe is so handsome. But he can't come with me now. I want to get some pictures of the fox family—if they're out—and he would not sit patiently and quietly while I wait for good shots.

When I turn the corner by the fox enclosure, the kits are out and chasing something small. A mouse, maybe? They are leaping and tumbling. I have to get these pictures. But I don't have any good patched holes on this side. I run to Dad's workshop for the pliers. I quickly cut a new hole and wriggle my camera lens in. I get shot after shot of the foxes leaping beside the mouse, which runs back and forth trying to escape the kits. They don't seem to want to kill it. But they sure do want to play with it.

Then I don't see the mouse any longer, and the kits lie down and rest for about twenty minutes. Nothing happens. That's okay. I'm getting used to waiting for shots to set themselves up. Finally, one of the kits bats its paw at the other, and they start to tumble. I adjust my shutter speed because I expect some more good action shots.

And I get them. The kits wrestle, playfully chew on each other's ears, and jump over each other like they have springs in their paws. I click as one on his back bats away another, who seems intent on playing leapfrog. The late-afternoon sun has again lit their fur in coppery splendor. I ought to write that down. Coppery splendor. Because that is really what it looks like.

A couple hours later, I am done. Time to repatch

the hole, this time the way Dad showed me.

But when I open the workshop drawer, I don't see any more patches. Oh no. I can't believe it! I can't catch a break today. I tie twine back and forth through the chicken wire to make a temporary patch and go inside to ask Sage for help.

Sage agrees to take me to the hardware store for patches. He agrees only after telling me I should have planned ahead. He's right: I should have planned ahead. Sometimes, I have such trouble thinking before doing.

Sage was already planning on driving me over to tonight's Vet Volunteer meeting. We're all sup- posed to bring our ideas about the abandoned ani- mals. I'm a little nervous because it doesn't seem like my ideas have made anyone happy lately.

In the car, I tell Sage a little about what's been going on with my friends. I don't tell him about going to the Photography Club meeting.

"And you don't understand why they might feel jealous?" Sage asks. He glances at me and back to the road.

"Jealous?" I answer. "I don't think anyone is jealous. They just don't understand."

"Well," he begins, "can you think of something you said or did to make them misunderstand?"

"I haven't done anything!" I say.

Sage doesn't say anything right away.

"Well," I say. "They think that because I went to the high school clubs and because I want all of us to do our reports there and want to move the Environmental Club meeting there, that I'm trying to leave them behind."

Sage slows at a STOP sign. He stops and looks in both directions then continues straight ahead.

"Are you trying to leave them behind?" he asks.

"Of course not." I look over at him. "They would come with me to the high school."

He nods slowly, and I can tell he is waiting for more of an answer than that. But I don't have any more of an answer.

"So, no idea?" he asks.

Now I am quiet. Maybe it would be good to figure this out with Sage before the meeting. It might help me to know what to say when I see Maggie and Zoe. Because they need to understand that this is not about them.

"You remember how lame middle school can be, right?" I ask. "You must remember how much better high school was when you finally got there, right? Well, that's what's going on, I guess. I'm just more ready for high school than my friends are."

"But you aren't going into high school yet. What's the rush?" he asks.

"Oh, Sage, you sound like Mom and Dad!" And Maggie, I think.

"Seriously, Brenna? High school isn't some magical place where you'll suddenly feel like a grown-up. And it can be stressful. More stressful than middle school.

"Come on," he continues, "that day you went to do the Photography Club thing? Remember, that was pretty stressful."

"Well, that's because I didn't know where I was going. That wouldn't have happened if I was a student there." I still don't tell him about my experience today. It's too embarrassing.

"But they weren't all nice and friendly to you, were they? Did any of them care that you were lost?" Sage stares straight ahead. "You know, the high school kids have some growing up to do, too. I don't think that exchanging your middle school friends for high school friends is the answer. I think you need to talk it out with your friends tonight. Sounds like this has been going on long enough to mess with a lot of people."

I think about that. It certainly has been hard on me. Maggie and Zoe, too, if I'm being honest with myself. Sunita has been pretty quiet about everything until lunch today. And David isn't as jokey and clueless as he lets on. And Josh and Jules are probably wondering what is going on. I guess this is a big mess.

We pull up to the clinic. Sunita's mom is pulling out of the parking lot. I see some of her other kids in the backseat. They all wave at us as they drive away.

"Thanks Sage, that helped," I say, getting out and standing beside Sage's car.

"No problem. Good luck. And hey, I'll find that hole and patch it for you." And Sage backs out of the parking lot, too. Finally, I get a break, and it comes in the form of my brother.

Inside, a couple of little kids wait with a bouncy wheaten terrier pup. The kids' mom has the pup on a loose leash so the puppy is bouncing and running between its owners and a few Vet Volunteers seated on the floor.

Josh and Jules sit cross-legged, and the puppy scrambles into each of their laps and back out again. Maggie looks up from the floor but doesn't say anything to me. She snaps her fingers above the puppy's head. The puppy keeps trying to lick them. This makes the two little kids laugh. They try to snap their fingers but don't know how. So one of the little boys moves his fingers pretending to snap, but he clicks with his tongue instead. Good idea. But the puppy goes for the source of the sound and licks the boy's mouth instead of his fingers.

This makes his brother roll on the floor laughing, and the puppy immediately joins him. The pup's leash gets tangled beneath the little boy. As the little boy tries to stand, the puppy runs back to Jules and the leash rubs through the little boy's fingers and he cries out in pain.

And that's when Dr. Mac calls the family in for the pup's checkup.

His mom hops up to help her son. "It's okay, Malik, it's just a scratch," she says. She holds his hurt hand and looks at it closely.

"But it's b-b-b-bleeding," he cries.

"Just a tiny bit," she says.

"We have bandages," Dr. Mac says. "Why don't you let my girls clean him up while we start with Finnegan? Maggie, Brenna, fix the little guy up and then bring him in to us, okay?" Dr. Mac does not wait for an answer. She takes the puppy's leash and heads to the Herriot Room.

The little boy's mom looks us over and must decide we can handle it because she allows us to take Malik to the Dolittle Room.

He has stopped crying, but he does not look as confident about us as his mom did. Maggie washes her hands and says to Malik, "We take care of all kinds of hurt animals in here. Puppies, kitties, we've even had a hurt snake here. Can you believe it?"

His eyes get round, and you can tell he's interested. Maggie dries her hands and puts on gloves. She nods at me to do the same. Jeesh, I was going to anyway. I wash, dry, and glove my hands.

"Can you bark like a tiny puppy?" she asks Malik.

"Ruff, Ruff!" he yells.

"No, a teeny-tiny puppy, like an almost-invisible puppy," she says. Maggie rinses his hand with sterile water over a basin.

"Ruff, ruff," he says in a soft, low voice.

"You are very good at that," she says to him.

From the human first-aid kit, I get a bandage and antibacterial ointment. We have to have a first-aid kit for us because we often get scratched up—or worse—by a frightened animal.

"Now a kitty," Maggie whispers. "A teeny-tiny, almost-invisible, little kitty." I hand her the bandage that I've already dabbed with ointment.

"Meow, meow, meow," Malik whispers.

Maggie places the bandage on his fingers. "All done," she says.

Malik smiles but then says, "Boring bandage."

Maggie looks at me.

"That's all we've got," I say apologetically. But then I remember something. "Just a sec."

I run out to the waiting room. I know where Sunita keeps the special stuff. Josh, Jules, Zoe, and Sunita are all out there.

"Just taking one," I say to Sunita when I close the desk drawer that we all call Sunita's. Even Dr. Mac.

Back in the Dolittle Room, I give the sheet of stickers to Maggie. She smiles—*smiles*—at me.

"Which one do you want on your bandage and which one do you want to keep?" Maggie shows him the stickers.

He chooses his stickers and asks, "Can I have one for my brudder, too?"

Maggie lets him choose another for his brother and walks him over to the Herriot Room. I throw out the bandage wrappings and use a sanitizing wipe on the exam table. All sterile for our next patient.

Maggie walks back into the Dolittle Room with Zoe right behind her. Maggie closes the door and says, "We need to talk."

Those are never good words to hear. She looks so uncomfortable. She looks like she might cry. Where did her smile from a moment ago go? Zoe looks from me to Maggie and back again.

"Before you say anything," Maggie begins, "I'm sorry I've been avoiding you. But I've been pretty mad. Well, hurt anyway."

I'm about to respond, but Maggie holds up her hand. She has more to say before she lets me talk.

"Look what a great team we make," she says. "Why would you want to break up a team?"

The exam room is clean, and there is nothing out of place, nothing to fix, nothing to do. We all seem uncomfortable, like we don't even know what to do with our hands, so we stand—Maggie and Zoe on one side, and me across from them— arms at our sides, the empty exam table between us.

"I don't want to break up the team. I don't know why you think that. Yes, I have wanted all of us to get to know some of the high school kids, but I didn't want that to mess things up between us."

I try to stay calm, although just saying those things makes me a little angry again. But it felt like old times for a moment there, and I want to go back to that. So I choose my next words carefully.

"Look, I've never had better friends than the Vet Volunteers. And I *love* being a Vet Volunteer."

I almost lean my hands on the sterile exam table, but then stop myself.

"But it sounded like you think you've outgrown us," Maggie insists. "That hurts, Brenna."

Zoe nods. She looks like she could cry.

"I don't feel like I've outgrown any of us," I say.

"Really?" Maggie says.

"Yes. Someday, I'd like to have a paying job and study abroad and, yes, go to high school. You, too. And I think you'd like some of these high school kids if you gave them a chance. Not all of them, but some."

"As long as they don't try to take away my best friend," Maggie says.

"No chance of that," I say.

"Hey, what about me?" Zoe asks.

"You're my best cousin," Maggie says, putting her arm around Zoe's shoulder.

"I guess I've been a little too focused on the next thing and not focused enough on the now thing, huh?"

"A little," Maggie says, and leans on the exam table."Now look what you did," I say. I hand Maggie and Zoe the wipes, and they laugh as we wipe away her handprints. Luckily, it's not so easy to wipe away our friendship.

Chapter Eleven

. . . .

By the time Dr. Mac is done with the well-puppy checkup, all the Vet Volunteers have made up and made some plans.

"Sorry, kids," Dr. Mac says after the family has left and she has locked the door behind them. "That took longer than I expected. First-time dog owners have lots of questions. I didn't realize they were first-timers, or I wouldn't have asked for you to come so early. She looks around at all of us seated on the floor and in the chairs of the waiting room.

"Did I miss anything?" she asks. Boy, did she ever.

"We had talked about doing high school presentations, but we've decided to drop those and put on a Community Awareness Day," Sunita pipes up.

I look at Maggie, then back to the group. "A spring open house at the wildlife rehabilitation center," I say. "We can show people around the center and teach people about the problem of abandoned animals."

Dr. Mac says, "Are your parents on board with this?"

"I haven't asked them yet. It just came together when all of us started talking," I explain.

"We could bring the bunnies that have been abandoned here," Jules suggests.

"Maybe some families would adopt them the day of the open house," Sunita says. "Especially if we advertise ahead of time that they're available. Give people time to consider the adoption. We don't want anyone doing this on impulse, after all."

"What if we called the shelter to see if they wanted to come, too?" David asks.

"You mean participate?" I ask him. "Maybe bring the bunnies that they have?"

"Yup. That's exactly what I mean," he says. "And, what if we invite the feed store and tractor-supply managers to come? They could learn about this problem. Might help for next year."

David can really surprise you some days. Inside that goofy brain of his lurk some pretty fantastic ideas.

"We could have the ducklings learn to swim," Maggie suggests. "People would come out to see what we mean, and they would have fun and a great lesson on what can happen to animals purchased as temporary toys."

"That's a great idea," I say.

"I got it from you," Maggie says.

"What?"

"When you did the presentation in science class. I listened," she says. I remember that she did. Even though she was so mad at me then, Maggie cares about animals and just eats up animal facts.

"Sounds like you kids have a lot of planning to do. Great ideas, all!" Dr. Mac says. Then she looks at me, "Brenna, you'll talk to your parents and get this nailed down?"

"Immediately," I say. I realize that it's a great opportunity to show them that I can be mature, and make up for some of the trouble I've caused recently.

That night, I e-mail all of the Vet Volunteers and give them the open house date, four Saturdays away. We have a lot to get done.

Four weeks later, we have a gorgeous day for the

wildlife rehabilitation center open house. In fact, it's so warm, it feels like a summer open house.

I walk around with Poe on my shoulder and my clipboard in my hand—it has all the times for the day's events in case someone asks me for them—and check on all our "stations."

I spot a reporter. She is carrying a large satchel and is holding a small notepad.

"Are you Brenna Lake?" she asks.

"I am."

"Nice to meet you. I'm Vivian Michael, *Montgomery County Gazette*? Your father—I believe it was your father—he's out there parking cars? He told me to come find you and I'd get a lot of good information? He said you'd be the one with a crow on your shoulder?" She smiles wide and nods her head up and down a lot.

She seems friendly. I like her. But it's kind of funny that everything she says sounds like a question even when she isn't asking anything.

"What would you like to know?" I ask.

"Well, I would like to know why you have a crow on your shoulder. But do you want to show me around? I can ask some questions as we go. Will that be all right?"

"We can start right here," I say. "We're calling this the Bunny Bungalow."

Jules and Sunita are in charge at this station. Their pop-up tent has no sides to it, just some shade over all the bunny cages and straw bales. Jules has the abandoned lionhead bunny on a bale of straw. Sunita has the tiny black bunny that someone left in a box outside Dr. Mac's Place. A couple of preschoolers wiggle around in front of the bunnies.

"Jules, Sunita," I introduce them, "This is Vivian Michael. She's a reporter."

"Hi," they say at the same time and then look at each other giggling.

"What can you tell me about these rabbits?" Ms. Michael asks. "They seem friendly."

Jules and Sunita look at each other. It seems like neither one knows who should talk first. I rescue them.

"Jules, maybe you can tell her about where all of these rabbits came from?" I can see Sunita relax a little. She smiles at Jules and pets the rabbit in front of her. While Jules tells about finding the rabbits, Sunita lets kids pet them. She and Jules have made bunny-care handouts. Sunita goes over one of the sheets with a mom and her two kids who drove an hour and a half to look at the bunnies for adoption.

"So what other questions do you have for me

about bunny care?" Sunita asks the lady.

"I think you've answered all my questions," she says. "I had rabbits my entire childhood. And now that my cat has died I think I'd like to have a rabbit again. My kids are so excited. I already bought a cage." Her kids nod and jump around a little. Their mom rests a hand on each of their shoulders, and they settle down with big grins plastered across their faces.

"Oh, so you've come prepared," Sunita says.

"I've been considering a bunny for the last year. When I saw the info about this open house and all the bunnies up for adoption, we just *had* to come."

Sunita and the mom continue to talk, while Sunita shows her all of the available rabbits. I listen again to Jules's conversation.

"I had no idea that people would just turn pet rabbits loose into the wild," Ms. Michael says, in horror.

Jules points out the poster she made, and David's, too. David's has great information, but the rabbit he drew looks a little like a pig.

Ms. Michael jots down a few more notes and turns to me and says, "I'm ready for our next stop."

I lead her to our Fox Family Station. Dad has built some temporary stockade fencing to shield the fox family from the visitors. Dad and Sage outfitted it with a hole—like a duck blind—so people can see the fox family but not get too near them or be seen by them. Sage is stationed there. He allows visitors to borrow his binoculars, and he explains how and why we care for animals like this fox family and how and when we release them back into the wild.

There is a line of about twenty people waiting to see through the binoculars. Sage was smart when he constructed a box for the smaller kids to stand on so they can see through the "duck blind," too. Everyone over here at Sage's station is also paying attention to the signs that say, PLEASE SPEAK QUIETLY, WE DON'T WANT TO FRIGHTEN THE FOXES.

Next, I take Ms. Michael to Mom in the critter barn. The family she has been talking with thanks her and leaves clutching Mom's handout. It shows what it takes to run our center. It has information in case people want to donate, volunteer, or even adopt a bunny. I introduce my mom to Vivian Michael.

"Nice to meet you," Mom says. "Brenna, I can show her the rest of the place so you can get ready."

I head off to find Maggie. Our presentation is set for two o'clock, and it's almost that time now.

I jog past Jayvee, crouching in the grass with a bunch of other kids. Jayvee has a special station set up to show off his origami dinosaurs, because what wildlife open house would be complete without the dinosaur display? Josh and a guy I recognize from the Outdoor Club are at a picnic table nearby helping kids make origami rabbits, ducks, and chicks. Jayvee helps them make dinosaurs. No one has abandoned any dinosaurs lately, but if they do, I know Jayvee will be on hand to tell them why they shouldn't.

The animal shelter's station is right near Jayvee's. They also have a pop-up tent and straw bales. A few families sit on the bales listening to the volunteer. The animal shelter has brought pictures of dogs and cats needing good homes. They also brought application forms. Every hour they give a presentation on adopting from the shelter as well as volunteering there. I looked at their photos earlier and thought I should consider volunteering my services. They could really use someone who can take better pictures than they have now. I bet they'd stand a better chance of having some of the animals adopted if people could see them clearer.

But I remind myself that I'm already doing plenty of volunteering. I can't do everything—especially if I want to do it right. And keep my friends. And that's when another idea comes to me, the Ambler

High School Photography Club. They could take on the animal shelter as a community service project. They could rotate volunteer photographers who go in and take photos of the animals in need of good homes. They'd certainly be better than the ones the shelter has now. But that club wasn't very nice to me. And honestly, I'm still too embarrassed to bring it up with them. I'll suggest this to Nick and let him talk to them instead.

Alongside my father's workshop, the Outdoor Club has set up a food stand. They're serving lemonade and cookies and, oddly enough, grilled asparagus. The asparagus is Zoe's idea. She's always trying to get everyone to eat healthier. Zoe stands behind the table with Nick and his girlfriend and Dr. Gabe. I recognize a couple of other boys from the Outdoor Club, too. One is arranging asparagus on a platter. Zoe seems to be assisting him in some way. I know it's not just because of her love for green vegetables. Typical Zoe. I don't think she can help herself.

Walking up to their table, I wave to Dr. Gabe, Nick, and his girlfriend.

"Hey, Brenna, great turnout!" Nick says. His girlfriend looks up from her phone.

"Sure is. Thanks for helping out," I say.

"I'm on call today, but I figured I'd hang around

here until I'm needed elsewhere. It's nice to see how well things are going," Dr. Gabe says. He and Nick continue their conversation.

"Hey, Zoe," I call, "any chance you know where Maggie is?"

"Haven't seen her since we set up the kiddie pool. Is she still over there?" Zoe asks.

She turns back to the boy she is "helping" without waiting for an answer from me. I just shake my head and continue on.

And then I see Maggie with a few adults heading my way. I recognize Mr. Kurt, manager of the feed store.

"Brenna, this is Mr. Morris from the tractor supply," Maggie says, introducing the other man.

I shake his hand. He looks at me strangely. Then I notice his eyes drift up. I had forgotten that I was still "wearing" Poe.

"Probably not used to a crow hanging around," I suggest.

"Not hardly," he replies. "Nice bird." He looks wary.

"Thank you," I say.

Mr. Kurt from the feed store says, "Now, I know I met you not long ago. With that rascally boy."

"Oh, David, he's actually really nice," I begin. "He just—"

"Don't take offense. I like rascally boys. Raised

four of them myself. He's in all the time with his dad. I like that kid."

"Thanks so much to both of you for coming. Maggie and I are about to begin our presentation," I say.

Maggie says, "Yeah, thanks." She points to my mom and the reporter heading our way.

"Good," I say to Maggie. "I wouldn't have wanted to start without them."

Maggie looks at the men and says, "Would you like to have a seat?"

She points to the rows of nearby straw bales. Some families are already settled in. Dr. Mac stands beside the easels that Maggie and I set up earlier. The kiddie pool is off to the left, and we are about ready to begin.

I smile at Maggie. She smiles and gives me a thumbs-up.

Dr. Mac begins, "Ladies and gentlemen, children, and animal friends, I'd like to introduce you to two of my Vet Volunteers. This is Brenna Lake and Maggie MacKenzie. They have a special presentation."

I hear a child in the front row stage whisper, "Is she a pirate?"

I motion to Dr. Mac to take Poe. I sometimes forget that not everyone expects to see a crow sitting on someone's shoulder. I don't want him to be a distraction from our presentation. I glance over at Maggie. She looks a little nervous.

I lean in and whisper, "You've got this. They're here because they want to know."

Maggie nods and begins. "One of the sadder parts of spring is the abandonment of Easter pets."

I flip the paper on the easel so everyone can see the first poster. It's the one Josh did. It shows an empty Easter basket and a bunny hopping away.

Maggie continues, "Every year, people buy rabbits, chicks, and ducklings as gifts for children. Most people do not realize the care that these pets need. Every year, people drop off these new pets the week after Easter to the animal shelter, the vet clinic, or to the dangers of the wild."

I flip the chart to show Maggie's poster on the statistics of how long these pets are expected to live in the wild before becoming prey to other animals, dying of starvation and hunger, or being killed in traffic.

The audience is hushed. The two store managers look concerned.

It's time for me to speak. Maggie flips the chart to reveal my poster. I give the same talk that I did for my science class. I tell people about the cruel practice of dyeing animals.

Now it's time for our duckling demonstration.

David and Josh lead the ducklings across the grass and through the crowd to us. The ducklings look like grown-up ducks now. At just five weeks, they are fully feathered, white Pekin ducks. Just like Dr. Gabe predicted. Maggie flips to the next poster of my photos of our first attempts at introducing the ducklings safely to water.

"Awww, so cute," I hear people say. And they are.

"Ducklings in the wild or born on a farm would have a mother to keep them safe and teach them what they need to know," I explain. "But ducklings that are sold in feed stores or tractor-supply stores or sold through the mail do not have mothers to help them."

I can see the two managers look nervous. I don't want to make them feel bad. But they need to know what happens.

I continue, "So if a farmer gets the ducklings, he or she knows what to do. But when people buy them for their children, the ducklings are in danger of drowning."

Some people gasp. I hear someone whisper, "That can't be." But Maggie and I continue. Maggie picks up a duck and points as I speak.

"At the base of their head, ducks have an oil gland. This gland excretes oil after the ducks have been submerged. If a duck was with its mother, she would make sure all her ducklings got out of the water after a dunking. Then the duckling would preen. They use their heads and wings to distribute the oils to all their feathers. Ducks are not waterproof until they have fully feathered out and have distributed the oils. A baby duck or duckling has fluff, not feathers. So they can become waterlogged and drown."

Again, I hear gasps. And someone says to another, "I had no idea."

"This is why so many baby ducks do not survive when they are given as gifts. Maggie and I did a lot of research. One of the things we found out is that many stores have a minimum number of six chicks and ducklings that a customer must buy, unless they already have a flock. This way, only farmers and families who want a backyard flock will buy the animals. So people aren't able to buy one or two as pets."

It's Maggie's turn again. This time she doesn't seem a bit nervous.

She says, "No animal should be thought of as a toy. These are living creatures. People should let the Easter bunny bring candy and stuffed animals and let the living creatures stand a chance at survival."

A couple little kids up front are very excited to hear the Easter bunny mentioned. They bounce up and down while sitting on their straw bales. The adults in the audience seem to agree with Maggie and me. I see many heads nodding. I hear bits of conversations.

But the store managers talk quietly to each other. I wonder what they're saying. Will they listen to us, even though we're just kids?

Chapter Twelve

· · · · · · · · · · · · ·

It is time for the big event, time to introduce the ducklings to the deeper water of the kiddie pool. Jules and Sunita have closed their station for a bit to see this. Zoe and a couple of the Outdoor Club kids have wandered over, too. I'd guess we have a crowd of over sixty people sitting on straw bales and standing in a big semicircle behind them.

I hope this goes okay. Maggie and I have been coached by my parents. They said it will be fine. Fun, actually. We've done our research. I just hope none of the ducks makes a run for it. I know they won't drown. That's the whole point here. I catch a glimpse of Sage in the back; he shoots me a thumbs-up. I look over at Maggie. She doesn't seem nervous in the slightest, just excited.

I identify the leader duck. It's the smallest one, a girl.

I tell the audience, "We can tell that this duck is a girl because she quacks. Only girl ducks quack. Boys whine. If you listen closely, you'll hear this one here whine today. Another way that we can tell he's a boy is because he has this extra tail feather. See this?"

Maggie points for me because she's closer to him.

"This tail feather that curls back toward his head shows that he's a boy."

A man in the crowd yells out, "If any of you can remember the 1950s, that's how the men's hairstyle 'ducktail' got its name."

Some of the older folks laugh a little and talk to each other about that. I'll have to look up a picture of this hairstyle. It sounds strange.

It's time. Maggie and I have piled stones beside the kiddie pool so the ducks can climb in and out. We've placed a big flat stone in the pool just to be sure that they have somewhere to rest if they have a hard time figuring out how to get out of the pool.

We have the paint tray beside the stones and the kiddie pool. We used it this week to get the ducklings familiar with the water. The three of them can't exactly swim in it. They are too big, and it is too shallow. But at least they are excited about the paint tray. At first they were scared of it.

It's time to splash in it so the ducks notice it.

Maggie splashes. She pats her hands on the water. The ducks notice but do not approach it. She splashes again. Nothing. The ducks lie back down on the grass. This won't be much of a show if they just hang around the grass for an hour.

I give the leader duck a little pat on her behind to send her to the paint tray. She stands and quacks but doesn't move. I pat her again, and she takes a few steps. The other ducks see her move, get up, and follow.

Finally, she's close to the paint tray. Maggie stops splashing and takes her hand away. The leader duck takes a couple more steps and then . . . gets in the paint tray. A few people clap and laugh. Then the other ducks follow her in, and everybody laughs. The three ducks are so big that while they are all in the paint tray, they are all also hanging out of it. They have outgrown their little body of water.

Now I show them the deeper water behind them. I lean over and splash like Maggie did in the paint tray. The ducks turn and look. But they do not move closer to it. Maggie shrugs. I try to pat

the leader duck toward this water now. She stands.
But instead of walking up the rocks and into the
big pool, she turns and runs the other way!

The other ducks follow her. Maggie and I follow the ducks. We can hear people laughing
behind us. The ducks slow and stop a few yards
away. Maggie and I slow down as well, then start
to creep up on them.

"What do you suppose we should do?" Maggie
asks.

"We need to get Lead Duck in that pool. The
others won't get in until she does," I say.

"So we walk them back and then what?"
Maggie asks.

"I'll get in with her," I suggest. "I'm wearing
shorts, so it's no big deal."

"You think that will work?"

"If she goes in, they'll go in. And we need to
make sure she goes in."

Now that we have a new plan, we walk the
ducks back to the pool. The littlest duck, our leader, walks out in front of the other two, quacking
away. When we get close to the pool, the ducks
hop back into the paint tray.

I kick off my sandals, step in the pool, lean over,
and snatch up Leader Duck. I hold her gently in
the pool. Gentle or not, she is unhappy. She quacks

loudly. The other two ducks hop out of the paint tray and run around and around the kiddie pool Everyone is laughing. I feel my face go red. Maggie is red, too. This was probably not such a good idea to do the swimming lesson so publicly.

But then, one of the ducks decides that he needs to be close to the leader. He turns and waddles up the rocks and right into the pool! The third duck paces back and forth in front of the pool as if trying to decide what to do. Finally, she gets into the pool, too.

It's time to dunk the ducklings. It seems a little mean, but it's the only way. I'm still holding the leader duck, and she's still quacking. I check to see if Maggie is ready. She nods at me. I loosen my hold on my duck's body and quickly push her head into the water. Maggie does it with the boy duck, and before I can dunk the third she dunks herself.

Immediately, the leader duck jumps out of the pool. She doesn't even need to use the rock stairs. The other two ducks also race out of the pool, but they both take the stairs. I step out of the pool, too. The ducks begin preening. They instinctively move their heads back and forth and raise and lower their wings, using their bills to move the invisible oil in and among their feathers. The audience members are all on their feet, watching the ducks do what comes naturally. And then the ducks do what ducks do best, they get right back into the pool and swim.

Everybody claps.

I say, "These ducks were lucky. They were found, cared for, and raised until they could safely do something that ducks ought to be able to do: not drown."

People clap again. The little kids in the front row look like they want to swim with the ducks, but fortunately their parents are making sure they do not.

"Thank you for coming today," I say. "We're still here for another hour and a half, so stop by all of our wonderful stations. And be sure and get some cookies and grilled asparagus."

I had to say it. It's just so weird. Zoe sticks out her tongue at me, real fast. But then she winks. We're good. Zoe and I. And Maggie and I? We're good, too.

David and Josh are careful not to come too close to the bathing ducks.

"That was great," Josh cheers.

"Yeah, especially the part when you both had to run after the ducks," David says, "That was my favorite part of the whole day."

"Gee, thanks, David," I say.

Maggie gives him a gentle push. He makes a big deal over falling on the ground and pretending to be in pain. Pure David.

"Hey, David," Josh says. "Did you tell them about Farmer Ziemian?

"Not yet," David says, getting up from the ground. "He's going to take the ducks. Great, huh?"

"That is great," Maggie says. "When?"

"Tomorrow," David says.

Wow, tomorrow. So soon. That is good news, even if it makes me a little sad. But then again, I'm always sad when any animal leaves the wild-life center.

I look around. Most people have gone back to the stations. A few people are heading for the parking lot. Dr. Mac and Dr. Gabe are talking to the two store managers. Dr. Gabe sees me looking their way. He lifts his chin slightly, and I have the feeling that we should go over to talk to them.

I lead the way.

Dr. Mac smiles and stands with her hands on her hips. She says to the managers, "These girls worked very hard on this event."

Maggie says, "We all did."

She looks at Josh and at David. Sunita, Jules, and Zoe have gone back to their stations, but Maggie is right. All of the Vet Volunteers worked hard.

Then Maggie adds, "We had some help today from a high school group, too."

Dr. Mac smiles. I do, too.

"I'm sure this rascally boy helped," the feed-store manager says, patting David on the shoulder.

Josh looks as if he might bust a gut trying to keep his laugh inside. His shoulders go up and down. David looks down. I can tell he's afraid he's going to laugh, too.

Dr. Gabe says, "Did you want to tell the kids your plan?"

The feed store manager looks at the tractor supply manager. He nods.

"Well, kids, we're going to take your advice. Next year, we will both insist on a minimum purchase of six chicks. That way, we can be sure that they're not going to be bought as disposable pets."

The tractor-supply manager nods his agreement.

"We really learned quite a bit from you kids today," the feed-store manager says. "Quite a bit. Oh, and no more dyed bunnies, either. I read the paperwork you sent over, young lady. You've opened my eyes."

David looks at me. I know he'll always keep my secret about what I *almost* did.

"Next year, we should do this again," David says. "But before Easter."

"Let's make it happen," the tractor-supply manager says. The Vet Volunteers look at one another. We really have made a difference today. I'm pretty sure that next year there won't be so many abandoned pets. It feels good.

We say good-bye to the store managers and help with the remaining stations. There is a lot to take down and put away for our next open house. Sage, Josh, and David stow the pop-up tents in Dad's workshop. Everybody else—including some of our friendly visitors—grabs the dozens of straw bales around and stacks them in the critter barn.

I say good-bye to my friends. Sage and I lead the ducks back to the critter barn where they will spend one last night. All the visitors are gone, and everything is back in order. I need something to eat, a shower, and bed.

After my shower, I find my family at the kitchen table. Piles of dishes sit in the sink and on the counter. They've been left for me: my punishment for poor patching and even poorer permission seeking. I'm on dish duty until July.

Plates of leftover cookies and asparagus sit next to a tray with a stack of fresh tomato sandwiches. I grab a sandwich. Jayvee has only cookies in front of him.

I wink at him. "Special day, huh?"

Jayvee smiles and takes a big bite out of his cookie. His whole body is swaying, so I can tell he's swinging his feet beneath the table. He is one happy camper. Sage shakes his head and laughs.

Mom and Dad flip through some of the prints I made. They look at the photos from when the fox family first came to stay with us, photos of the ducklings' first day at Dr. Mac's, and photos of my friends. In a second pile are the origami dinosaur photos. They are so very cool.

Mom pats the dinosaur pile. "I can't believe the effect you were able to achieve," she says.

"I'll have the frames done this week so we can get them up in Jayvee's room," Dad says.

Jayvee beams, and those legs keep swinging.

Until Mom says, "Jayvee, please. Table manners."

Jayvee stops swinging but not smiling. "Thanks, Brenna," he says. "My dinosaurs look like real paper dinosaurs."

We all laugh. "They do look like real paper dinosaurs," I say.

Dad turns a photo around so that I can see it. It's one of the fox kits. I used the same photo last month in my slide show for the Outdoor Club. That seems like so long ago.

Dad says, "Brenna, this is stunning. You were always good, but over this past year, you have become a truly amazing photographer. The action, the lighting, how did you learn to do all this?"

"Thanks," I say. I feel my face going red. "I'm always reading about technique and composition. And I just go outside and try."

"I wonder where this might take you." Dad says softly as he flips through a couple more photos.

Sage pulls a picture of the ducklings from the stack. The ducklings are tiny, practically round balls of bright yellow fluff.

"That was when we first found them, remember?" I ask him.

"You forget how small they were, don't you?" he says.

"They grow so fast," I say. Sage pulls out a picture from a couple weeks later. The ducklings' necks look longer, and their bodies not so compact.

Mom has gotten up from the table and returned with the family photo album. Oh no, this can make my parents sappy for hours.

"Just look at how fast they grow," Mom says, pointing. The first few photos are of Baby Sage. He looks tiny, but you can see those same intense eyes. In the background, our cabin looks new and uncluttered. Not much furniture around, either.

Mom keeps flipping, Sage grows older, and we

get to me as a baby. Okay, I was seriously cute. My brown hair is soft and curly. Mom must have had a thing for weird baby headbands. I'm wearing a different one in almost every picture. Some pictures are of me alone, some with Mom or Dad, but most are just Sage and me.

Dad says, "That doesn't seem so long ago." He is pointing to my first day of school picture. I look determined in my red plaid jumper and blue shoes.

It seems a long time ago to me. I can't remember that picture being taken. I can't remember the dress or the shoes. I do remember the Dora the Explorer backpack I am clutching. But otherwise, kindergarten, and almost all of elementary school, is a bit of a blur. Sometimes it feels as if I've been in school forever.

Then Mom turns a page, and there is Baby Jayvee. He is sitting in his high chair covered with spaghetti. It's in his hair, all over his face, and smeared across the high chair tray. He's laughing. And swinging his feet. I look over at Jayvee. I do remember when that picture was taken. Mom turns the page, and five-year-old Jayvee is standing on the same spot I was for his first day of school. Not only do I remember that picture being taken, but it really seems as if it was only months ago.

How can this be? It doesn't feel like anything has sped by for me. And Sage pretty much seems the same. But Jayvee? Jayvee's life seems to be moving faster than ours. I look over at him. I realize I still think of him as a four- or five-year-old. He's still a kid, but he's a kid who can make origami dinosaurs. A kid who can climb trees and do multiplication. He's growing up almost as fast as a duckling. For the first time ever, I think I want the world to slow down.

Chapter Thirteen

. . . .

At first, Sage was going to take just Maggie and me to Farmer Ziemian's to release the ducks. But Zoe heard that Sage was driving and wanted in. No problem, there; Zoe brings the fun with her, after all. Everyone else is working at the clinic today. I've brought my camera so we'll be able to tell—and show—them all about it.

When we get to the farm, Farmer Ziemian points to the pond. It's beyond the empty pasture and right before the rye field. Sage stays behind to talk to Farmer Ziemian about his sustainable farming techniques, and we girls head to the pond.

We take turns carrying the crate. The ducklings take up so much more room in the crate than they did a month ago. It isn't exactly heavy, but it is awkward. Besides that, the ducks keep scooting back and forth, shifting the balance of the crate.

"I thought he said this was an empty pasture," Zoe says. She is taking tiny steps and slowing us down.

"Doesn't it look empty to you?" Maggie says. "No cows, no sheep, no nothing."

I look around. What is Zoe talking about? Maggie is right. No animals, only scrub plants from when the previous animals chewed it down.

"There is dried manure everywhere!" Zoe says.

Maggie rolls her eyes. "Somebody should have worn the right shoes," she says.

"Well, how was I to know we'd be stomping through manure?" Zoe looks before taking her next tiny step.

I don't see all this manure she's so afraid of. But then, I wore my barn boots, so I'm all set.

Maggie shakes her head. "Did you think the pond would be surrounded by a paved parking lot?"

"I wasn't really thinking much about it at all. I just thought it would be fun for us to spend some time together with Sage and the ducks," Zoe says.

Maggie shoots me an amused look. I think we both know this was a flirting expedition for Zoe. Oh well. It comes with the package.

When we finally get to the edge of the pond,

we search for a place to sit. High reeds and grasses surround most of the pond, but there is a nice little "beach" section, as well. A few big flat stones dot the area, giving us a place to sit with clear views of the entire pond.

The pond is large. I would have called it a small lake. Trees shading the far side and lily pads dot the shore closest to us. I set the crate down, Maggie opens it, and the ducks file out behind their little leader. She looks back and quacks at me. I wonder if she is telling me off for putting her in a crate again.

We laugh and watch the ducks head for the water. But they stop before they get too far. The leader lies down, so the others do, too. They sample some of the tall grasses and cast glances at the water.

"Do you think we should give them a pat like we did when we waterproofed them?" Maggie asks me.

"I think we should wait. Give them a little time to adjust."

Zoe picks a tall, slender stalk of grass. She puts it between her thumbs and blows. The whistle sounds like a train.

Maggie says, "Where'd you learn to do that?"

"I have all kinds of hidden skills," Zoe says. She

wets her lips and whistles through the grass again.

"Teach us," Maggie says.

We practice positioning the grass like Zoe shows us, but neither Maggie nor I quite get the hang of it. Ours sound more like the whine of a boy duck than a train. We watch the ducks get closer to the water's edge, and the three of us whistle in our own ways. Maggie gets pretty close. But her whistle is higher and inconsistent.

Mine generally sounds like I'm just spitting. Every once in a while a tone comes out, but then I need to take a breath and I'm spitting again.

Maggie puts down her stalk. "You know, your friends from the Outdoor Club are pretty cool. Yesterday, they taught me a few compass skills. And they showed me how to identify some edible plants at the edge of the woods."

"I'm glad you liked them," I say.

"The boys from the Outdoor Club are especially nice," Zoe says with a smile. "They thought serving grilled asparagus was brilliant."

"I'm sure they did," Maggie says, rolling her eyes once more. I look at the cousins. They are so different from each other and yet such a perfect pair.

The ducks are on the water's edge now, dipping their bills in but otherwise staying dry. Baby steps, I guess.

I turn to Maggie and Zoe. "I really am sorry for making you think I was choosing those high school kids over you. I would never do that. I couldn't ask for better friends than you guys. Than all of the Vet Volunteers."

"That's okay," Maggie says. "We get it now. Some high school kids are cool."

"I know I'm impatient. I'm ready for whatever's next, and I want to drag you all along with me."

"You're not impatient when it comes to your picture taking. Especially your wildlife photos."

That's true. I'd never really considered that before.

"Have you ever heard of playing to your strengths?" Maggie asks.

I shake my head no.

"It's what my basketball coach teaches us," Maggie begins, "In a game, Coach has us play the positions we're best at. Take the shots we're good at. In practice, she has us start with what each of us does best and then work on what needs to improve. It helps with confidence. And it helps the whole team out if each one of us plays to our strengths."

"Okay, I get that. But what does it have to do with me?" I ask.

Zoe looks as if she doesn't completely understand, either.

Maggie says, "When you get a new idea, you want to drag us along with you. That's usually a good thing. You make us jump in and find out about something we don't know. That's playing to your strengths."

"Yeah, well, sometimes I make you pretty miserable with that. Moving everybody too fast," I say. I wonder where Maggie is going with this.

"But we're playing to our strengths, too. We ask questions. Sometimes we put the brakes on you. You take the harder shot. It's good for the team."

"I get it," Zoe says. "We make Brenna work harder and figure things out more before she leaps, right?"

"Yup!" Maggie says. "We all improve. You drag us forward. In the end, it's a good thing."

Wow. Maggie has been doing some pretty deep thinking about this.

I try my grass whistle again and then wipe the spit off my mouth and say, "We'll all be up at the high school soon enough, anyway. Middle school is flying by."

Zoe nods her head. "Before you know it, we'll all be away at college and then doing whatever it is we're going to do with our lives. What do you guys want to do?"

I ask, "You mean, what do we want to be when we grow up?"

We all laugh at that lame question. Adults seem to ask it whenever they don't know what to say to you. But today, beside the big pond, it's a very good question.

"I wanna be a vet like Gran. I want to work with her here. School is hard for me though. College and vet school are going to be tough."

"You'll do it," I say. When Maggie wants something, she works hard to make it happen.

I look at Zoe. "How about you?" I ask.

"I want to be a fashion designer. Or an actress like my mom," she says, striking a pose.

"I thought you would want to be a chef," I say.

"No, no, I want to be an actress or a fashion designer, and when I go on talk shows I will wow them with my culinary skills. And then I'll write a celebrity cookbook. I've got it all planned," Zoe boasts.

"I guess you do," I say. Zoe talks as if the matter is settled. No doubts at all. I wish I were like that.

"And you?" Maggie asks, looking at me.

"I really don't know," I say. "Help my parents

run the rehab? Become a science teacher, maybe. I'm not sure."

Maggie and Zoe look at each other with puzzled expressions.

"What?" I ask.

"Everyone thinks you're going to become a wildlife photographer," Maggie says.

"A famous one," Zoe adds.

Everyone thinks this? Who is everyone? I've never considered it.

"Can you really be a wildlife photographer as a job?" I ask. "Are there people who can make enough money to live on?"

"Why wouldn't there be?" Maggie shrugs. "I don't know. Google it."

"I will. If we know nothing else about my strengths, we know I'm a good researcher."

We laugh again and then look out at the pond. The ducks are in the water. We missed the moment when they actually got in. But doesn't that seem to be the way things go? It's hard to know when the new thing starts. You often realize it only when you've gone far enough to look back a little and know that you've moved on.

The three ducks paddle close by us and then finally set out for the far shore.

Turn the page to read a chapter from another exciting Vet Volunteer adventure!

Chapter One

. . . .

I still think you need a cat, Sunita," Zoe tells me as we bounce along in the school bus. We're going to Dr. Mac's Place, the veterinary clinic where we volunteer. It's the perfect way to start the weekend.

"Forget about it," I say. "It's useless. My mother won't let me. End of story."

"You're giving up too easily." Zoe fixes the butterfly clips in her hair. "You like cats more than anyone I know."

She has a point. I've always loved cats. Long-haired, short-haired, tabby, Siamese, or stray. I adore them all. I can watch cats for hours—the graceful way they move, that mysterious look in their eyes, the twitching tail, the cute whiskers— everything about them fascinates me.

My mother, however, doesn't like them. I think they scare her, though she won't admit it. Instead, she gives reasons like "They shed" or "They'll ruin the furniture with their claws." She has made up her mind. No cats in the Patel house.

"You just haven't asked the right way," Zoe continues. "Parents expect you to ask a million times so they know you really, really, really want something. You've probably only asked, like, a thousand times."

Zoe's mother is an actress. I'm sure she doesn't mind if Zoe gets a little dramatic when she wants something. That doesn't work at my house.

"My mother isn't the kind of person who likes being asked a million times for anything," I explain. "She's a doctor. She wants facts."

Zoe's redheaded cousin, Maggie MacKenzie, leans across the aisle. "The fact is you're great with cats and you deserve a pet," she says.

David Hutchinson turns around in the seat in front of us. "Tell your mom that a cat would eat the mice in your basement," he says.

"Yuck!" Zoe protests. "That's disgusting."

Brenna Lake, sitting next to David, punches his arm lightly. "Sunita doesn't have mice, you bean head." She twists around to face Zoe and me. "Write down all the reasons why you want a cat and give the list to your mom. Make sure you have lots."

"I doubt that would work," I say with a laugh. "My mother wants a cat that doesn't have fur, claws, or teeth, or need a litter box or food. In other words, she'll let me have a stuffed animal."

"But she let you volunteer at the clinic," Maggie says. "Remember how much that surprised you? Maybe you should give her a chance."

She's right about that. I didn't expect Mother to let me volunteer with the others. But she did. At first I thought helping at the clinic would be enough. If I got to be around cats at Dr. Mac's Place, I wouldn't want one of my own so badly. But being around them makes me want one of my own even more. There has to be something I can do to get Mother to change her mind.

The bus slows as we approach our stop.

"OK, you guys," I say, turning to my friends. "You've convinced me. I'll try asking mother again. But I have to find the right way to do it. Now let's get to Dr. Mac's Place."

Dr. Mac's Place is run by Dr. J.J. MacKenzie, Maggie and Zoe's grandmother. We call her Dr. Mac. She invited Brenna, David, and me to volunteer at the clinic with Maggie and Zoe last month, and it's the most spectacular thing that has ever happened to me.

Being at the clinic is amazing. We see all kinds of animals, from cats to canaries, puppies to potbellied pigs. My favorite parts are when the veterinarians let us help them during examinations and when we learn about things like X-rays and blood tests.

It's not always fun, though. Some of the work is boring and smelly, like cleaning cages or mopping floors. But every job is important—that's what Dr. Mac says.

Since my dream is to be a vet when I grow up, I'll do whatever she asks. I want to know everything I can about animals. Especially cats. Whenever I have any free time at home, I devour the cat books that Dr. Mac lets me borrow, or surf the Internet to find Web sites about cats.

All this reading may explain why Socrates likes me. Socrates is huge. Twenty pounds of muscle and attitude. His fur is a blend of orange, rust, and yellow that reminds me of apricots. You can see faint stripes on his tail. I bet he had a tabby cat for a grandfather.

Socrates has the reputation of being an aloof, "worship but don't touch me" cat. Maggie says that he rarely lets her pet him or pick him up. He likes to sleep on Dr. Mac's desk or on the receptionist's counter, but he takes off if anyone tries to scratch under his chin or between his ears.

That's why Maggie and Dr. Mac were so surprised when Socrates hopped into my lap a few weeks ago. He had never done that to anyone else before. It's like he picked me to be his favorite human. He always walks up to me when I enter the clinic and lets me pet him for a few minutes. If I sit down, he sits with me. Maggie thinks he likes the smell of my shampoo. (I have long black hair, and he does like to play with it.) Dr. Mac says he cuddles with me because I'm a calm and quiet person.

I have a different idea. Socrates knows how much I want a cat of my own. He can tell that I love him. I think he's adopted me. I guess I've adopted him, too. I've adopted him in my heart. He's like my pet away from home—until I get my own.

We round the corner, and Dr. Mac's Place comes into sight. Dr. Mac's house is a two-story brick building with dark green shutters and a matching green door. The clinic pokes out of the left side of the house, a one-story addition. It has its own door and two windows that face the street. A garden of spring flowers blooms along the entire front of the building. Dr. Mac says that animals enjoy flowers just as much as people do.

Socrates shoulders his way out of the daffodils to greet me as we get closer. He butts his head against my shins, and I crouch down to pet him.

"Hello, Socrates!" I say.

He purrs loudly, like a lawn mower engine, and rubs the corner of his mouth against my knuckles. Cats have special scent glands on their faces, and when they rub against a person like this, it's a way of marking their territory. It's kind of nice that Socrates thinks I'm part of his world.

"You should feel how warm his fur is," I tell the others as I lay my hand on his back. "I bet he's been lying in the sun all afternoon."

"Cats have all the fun," David says. "Eat, sleep. Eat, sleep, sleep, sleep. Eat some more. Wish I could do that."

"Hey, look!" Zoe says, pointing to the corner

of the yard. "Another cat. Do you think Socrates has a girlfriend?"

The new cat steps delicately onto the grass and walks toward us. It's a tuxedo cat, mostly black with white paws and a patch of white on her chest. It's easy to see this is a she-cat. She's very pregnant, with a heavy belly that almost touches the ground.

Socrates stiffens and growls. I can feel the vibration of his warning call under my fingertips. He doesn't want her here, and he's telling her she should leave.

"Shh," I say quietly. "She's not going to hurt you. Just relax and be friendly."

Socrates is not in the mood to be nice. He steps away from me to face the black cat, his ears flat against his head. His tail whips back and forth, warning the other cat.

"Hisssss!"

It looks like fur is going to fly.